The Taroona Incident

Elizabeth Long

First published by Busybird Publishing 2022

ISBN
978-1-922691-47-7 (print)
978-1-922691-48-4 (ebook)

Cover image: Atahan Demir - Pexels
Cover design: Busybird Publishing
Layout and typesetting: Busybird Publishing

Busybird Publishing
2/118 Para Road
Montmorency, Victoria
Australia 3094
www.busybird.com.au

To my grandparents Emily and Charles.

Always remembered.

We respectfully remember the MUWININA
whose homelands we now live upon here
in Taroona. We are grateful for their care of
the land and for the deep knowledge their
descendants carry.

The name Taroona is said to derive from the
Aboriginal word for the chiton, a marine
mollusc found on rocks in the inter-tidal and
shallow sub-tidal regions of our beaches.

Contents

Chapter 1

The Present

It was overcast but mild and warm, a pleasant day for catching up on exercise. Her pace was not too fast, unlike the sweating, pained faces of the runners who passed her. She took in the sounds and scents of early spring and drank it in as if it would rejuvenate her lagging spirits. Melancholy was never too far away.

She enjoyed the freedom of a walk. It enabled her to see the changing scenes without personal involvement. Here there was no need for commitment, no burdening responsibility, no awkward conversation or grinding competition, just simple observation from a distance.

The walking path ran parallel with the busy main road but occasionally it cut through small areas of grassy reserve where the trees had been mercifully left intact. Large groups of corellas took flight at her approach and landed again after she moved on. Their shrill, noisy chatter momentarily dominated all else until they resumed their search for food in the grasses. Further along the path was a small group of buildings stretching beyond the petrol station. Sunday was always busy here.

There was a nursery with row upon row of brightly painted terra cotta pots of various sizes, and a woman putting new plants into a car boot while excited children ran amok in the car park. Her husband stood awkwardly, handing over the plants one by one while shouting at the children, who were dodging reversing vehicles, people and bikes. Pandemonium in a peaceful place. Sand, Mulch, Stone & Soil was next door, a blur of dust and motion as soil and gravel was moved from one place to another. Loud music played, cigarettes hung from sweaty mouths, gears crunched through scarred, rusty machinery, men doing what men do. A constant stream of trailers being filled to the brim with the foundation of somebody's dream of paradise in the suburbs. Further along, on four acres, proudly sat Country Receptions. Catering for weddings and parties. Open seven days a week. Visitors welcome.

Two white Mercedes with shivering white ribbons pulled into the driveway in front of her, halting her progress, the cars carrying yet another wedding party. Slowly and deliberately the entourage moved up the driveway to the little chapel and reception rooms specifically designed for the purpose. In the centre of the manicured gardens the fountain was spitting water high into the air from small, concrete-carved boys' mouths. Ducks on the pond swam and dived as if on cue. The bride smiled, immaculate, fresh, young. She sat upright and immobile, not wanting to disturb the perfect picture of a flawless bride for the guests to admire. It reminded her of a little plastic figure on a wedding cake. *You're a cynic*, she thought.

This was an ordinary suburb in transition. Every old dwelling was under siege and doomed as soon as the For Sale sign was slammed into the soil. The speed of the transformation always amazed her. Sold one day, house demolished the next and six new units squashed onto the block before anyone could scream a word of protest. Brick squares, some with half of the walls rendered, a balcony attached here and there. All came with compact clotheslines and little patches of instant lawn. Huge boards outside the finished product advertised a new lifestyle with three bedrooms, walk-in robes, study, modern kitchen and courtyard all close to shops, transport and schools.

She was nearly halfway through her walk. Someone had told her that thirty-five minutes, three times a week was enough to keep weight off. Not that weight was a problem. She was still slim for her age. Women often taunted her about it, as if she had purposely set out to betray her sisters by remaining thin. It was usually friendly banter, done in a rare quiet moment in the office.

'I was starved as a kid.'

'Sure. How much exercise do you do?'

'Hardly any, I smoke too much.'

'It's sex then.'

'Absolutely.'

She turned her attention back to her walking pace, looked ahead and checked the time. The path started to wind back into the part of the walk she enjoyed the most. A pleasant, larger slice of reserve with tall native bushes and trees. Sometimes she would just stand still, listening to anything that moved. A quick, short breeze moving among the branches, the screech of a cockatoo. Something in this place reminded her of early childhood; then she would snap out of it, move on.

It was unusually quiet on this part of the walk today. *Weird*, she thought. A quick, short gust of wind made her shudder. *Better get back.*

Papers were blowing across the path up ahead. Too many for her to ignore. She walked towards them, hoping to pick up a few before it all got out of hand. As she approached, she became aware of a small, white terrier sitting beside a body, motionless. Her ears started ringing, so loudly nothing else penetrated this strange space she had entered. She was suddenly cold, the trees didn't bend in the wind, the birds had flown away, everything had become suspended. The body didn't move, panic was creeping up on her, she tried to contain it, smother it, talk herself out of it, but it clung to her like a wet, cold towel. She forced herself to get closer, fighting every sense that said run, run.

There was a tall figure of an old woman under a mass of soggy papers; the dog had been trying to free itself from the tangled lead held tightly by its owner. A small trolley lay on its side, cover off, revealing a few grocery items and more papers slowing succumbing to the puddles of water created by last night's downpour. Then she saw blood turning the woman's hair a dull red. She wanted to be sick. She touched the shoulder of the woman, softly, trying to tell if she was breathing. She cursed herself for being inadequate. The dog didn't move, just stared, resigned. She put her hand in front of the woman's face.

Was that a breath?

Not sure, not sure, probably the wind.

Oh God, where is everyone?

A young woman was running down the path.

'Please, can you help me?'

The small crowd parted to let the ambulance through. The old woman was alive but had a head injury, probably from falling they said. Two men worked on her, asking for her name, testing for vital signs. Certain she could be moved, she was bandaged and carefully put on a stretcher. A tube was coming from somewhere joined to a plastic bag one of the medics was holding above his head. For the first time, she was able to see all of the woman's face as she passed by. The silence came again, she felt sick, then it subsided.

She looked down; she had the dog, the lead still in her hand and the dog was looking at her.

Chapter 2

'Where have you been? I was just about to come looking for you … What's this?'

Rebecca held on to the dog.

'Are you alright?' Andrew asked, noticing her distress.

'Yes, yes, I will explain in a minute. I'm going to give it some water.'

He followed her outside. She filled up a container. The little dog drank and drank, relieved itself then ran back inside, jumped onto a chair and went to sleep. Maybe the dog was traumatised or exhausted. She covered it and they went to make coffee.

Andrew Amos waited; he was like that, he would just wait. He had waited for Rebecca to make up her mind to marry him, he waited for his son to grow out of his rebellion, he waited for clients to call back, he waited for colleagues to call back. He just waited.

Sometimes this infuriated her. She wanted to shake him.

'Call them.'

'No.'

'Why?'

'No point in putting the pressure on, they either like me or not.'

'Sell yourself.'

'My designs do that.'

'Christ, Andrew …'

They had gone through hard times lately. His business had slowed and he was forced to apply for a position with other architects. It could not have been easy for him. She always berated herself after grilling him like that, left her feeling ugly and nagging.

'I'm really envious of your calm and strength,' she once admitted to him during a solemn conversation.

'Yeah? Well, I'm jealous of your bum and your money,' he replied with a grin.

This was the second marriage for both of them and after seven years they still liked each other.

He was still waiting for her to say something. He poured the coffee, she poured the milk.

'You're shaking.'

'I know.'

'Don't tell me, you met some Amazonian Neanderthal while out walking, he knocked you off your feet and you're leaving me. The dog's a goodbye present.' He was smiling, trying to help her. He put his arm around her. 'Ok, what happened?'

She poured it all out, feeling relief, gripping the coffee cup, letting the warmth flow through her.

'It was frightening, Andrew. It wasn't just the body it was something else, I can't explain it, some sort of deep fear from out of nowhere.'

He held her again. 'It's alright, love, you're alright.'

'I felt so bloody inadequate.'

'You handled it fine. How did you come to bring the dog home?' Slight admonishment in his tone; he knew she always wanted one.

'I picked it up because it was shivering.'

He had a look of doubt.

'Well, no one seemed to care what happened to it, the police didn't ask, they just wanted to know my name and address.' She was on the defensive. 'After they finished with me, I started to walk home, I was so deep in thought I forgot to hand the dog back.'

'What do you want to do with it?'

'Well, let's keep it for now and see what happens,' said Rebecca.

'Ok, I'll call the police later and ask. Maybe the dog can stay until it's better. Mark is coming for dinner tonight.'

'Oh God! Forgot, sorry.'

'Would you like me to cancel?' Andrew asked.

'No, please, let's have some normalcy.'

They smiled.

Mark worked for an airline; his life was anything but normal. He would entertain them for hours with stories of passengers and crew. His current position was an interim measure. Ultimately, he wanted to join the police force.

'Alright. We'll have takeaway, I'll go and order it. We need food for the dog anyway. Pour a glass of wine, I'll ring Mark.'

'Do you think he'll mind?'

'Missing out on your cooking, you mean?'

'Very funny.'

She poured two glasses, took hers and went to look at the dog. It was still sleeping, making quiet yelping sounds. She wondered if it was a joyful dream or a nightmare. She stroked it. It opened its eyes, looked at her, then went back to sleep. She sipped her wine listening to Andrew tell his son of the day's events.

'No, she would love to see you … No, fine, yes, that ok with you? … Great, see you later.'

There was never any doubt about the love he had for his son. It was a joy to see his face light up at the prospect of spending some time with him. Made her regret not having children.

Andrew took a gulp of his wine.

'He's still coming then?'

'Yep. Feeling alright?'

'Much better. I'll have a shower.'

The wine was taking effect and all the fear had left her. 'Is he bringing a girlfriend for you to ogle?' she teased. This was an ongoing joke between them.

'No,' he said, sticking out his bottom lip in mock disappointment. He smiled at her and grabbed his keys.

While she was in the shower the dog came in and stayed until she had finished.

Mark turned up with yet another exotic bottle of wine and more tales. He resembled his mother. Fair, green-blue eyes, sharp features, quite handsome. He seemed physically strong without looking overly muscular. He was far kinder to Rebecca tonight, perhaps sensing her fragility.

'What are you going to name the dog?' he asked, after he had exhausted his repertoire of gossip.

'Um … well, because this is only temporary, I hadn't even thought about it.'

'You seem disappointed.'

'Well, I am. We seem to have become attached already.' She smiled.

'Male or female?'

She picked it up. 'Female.'

He took it from her and examined for himself, then patted and settled the bewildered little terrier on his lap.

'You like dogs then?' she asked, surprised at his careful tendering.

'Love them.' He exhaled cigarette smoke. It floated up towards the ceiling light. 'Not home long enough to have one though, wouldn't be fair. Remember Rex, Dad?'

'Yes, great dog.'

'You didn't tell me about that,' she reproached him.

'I forgot, really. It was a long time ago. Mark kept badgering us. We finally went to the local dog home, just to have a look,' he glanced at Mark pretending irritation, 'and came home with a year-old black lab. He turned out to be a very personable being and we became devoted. Rex died about six years later. Cancer.'

There was silence while Andrew and his son remembered and mourned their loss.

It seemed emblematic to Rebecca and she wondered if it was the catalyst for the departure of Mark's mother. Apparently, on one of those hot summer days when everything seemed right with the universe, she simply stated she had had enough, organised her things and in a week was gone, leaving her two males behind. The following months must have been a tortuous journey. Mark was sixteen, fragile, rebellious and Andrew bewildered and damaged. Two years later Mark reconciled with his mother and Rebecca was in his father's life. She suspected Mark resented her. Perhaps the son saw her as the Hadrian's Wall on the insurmountable hill, the final bastion that prevented a reunion he had dreamed of. His approach to her always seemed measured and contrived. She was resigned to this lack of connection.

'Bec, Bec, are you alright?' Andrew asked. 'You're looking a bit pale.'

They were now focused on her.

'Yes, fine, sorry, miles away. Coffee?'

'Love one. I'll organise the tape?' They had decided to watch a movie.

Mark gently put the dog down. 'I'll help you,' he offered, following her into the kitchen. She was unused to this attention from him.

They started sorting dishes and leftovers, putting the kettle on, getting out the cups, with no conversation and then:

'You had an unusual experience today.'

'Yes, bit of a shock.'

'Do you know what happened?'

'Not really, I think she just fell over.' She was hesitant in sharing her feelings. 'I came across all this while out walking and—'

'Hey! Come and look at this.' Andrew was calling from the other room. 'Quick, you'll miss it.'

The short newsbreak was airing and some beautiful face was listing the day's tragedies.

'Ms Taylor, a former prominent news reporter, was responsible for revealing the scandal that led to the sacking of two federal ministers. Hospital sources say she is recovering in intensive care after complications caused by the fall and is reported to be in a stable condition. There are no suspicious circumstances. And now for the weather …'

'Is that her?' asked Andrew.

'Who?'

'The woman you came across today.'

'Didn't recognise the face in the photo. How do you know it was the same person?' asked Rebecca.

'News cameras must have been there after the ambulance left, they showed the place where it happened, called us an outer-Eastern suburb.' He found it amazing that his wife had been involved with someone rather famous.

'Do you remember that incident?' he asked rather excitedly.

'Vaguely.'

'Two ministers were accepting bribes from CCR Constructions. Consequently, CCR won the right to open up and develop government land along the peninsula, you know, put up housing, jetties, shops, infrastructure, that sort of thing. It was big time, big money. I remember it because a mate of mine worked for a particular architectural firm who were asked by CCR to consider doing some design work for the project. They nearly took it on too, but this business was exposed before it all got started. One of the ministers committed suicide.'

Rebecca still struggled to remember all the details of that event in 1978.

Andrew continued on. 'I used to read her articles. She was controversial for her time, well-travelled, reported from all over the world. Corruption in governments was a pet hate of hers. She was a brilliant researcher, had a talent for sniffing out the facts. Nothing got past her. Tough lady.'

'You have a better memory than I do, darling.' She smoothed down his hair and kissed his cheek.

The three of them settled into their favourite places to watch last week's second-best offering from the television movie lineup, but Rebecca retired halfway through. The day had been unsettling, tiring.

Their bedroom faced out onto a small paved courtyard. They had worked hard on this area of garden. It was a perfect square and they had planted its boarders with azaleas. In spring and summer, the colours were breathtaking. She lay on her side and looked out the window, her eyes slowing adjusting to the blackness. A strong breeze was forcing the leaves in different directions as if against their will and she absent-mindedly watched the struggle. The men's laughter filtered into the room from the other side of the house. Father and son enjoying each other's company. There was something moving along the bed, quietly, deftly. After shuffling and sniffing and pawing at the blankets, the dog finally settled. She liked its company.

Chapter 3

The Past

The child woke up screaming. Lights went on and her grandparents rushed to her.

'What's wrong, pet? What's wrong?'

Her grandmother pulled her out of the sheets and wrapped her in her arms almost smothering the child with her large breasts.

'There's a spider.'

'Where, darling? Where?'

'I'll get it,' her grandfather cheerfully offered. He took off his leather slipper, banged the miniature creature on the wall, looked down to the carpet and pronounced it dead.

'Is it gone now?' Rebecca asked her grandfather, her bottom lip still quivering.

'Yes, love, it's gone.'

Assured, she crawled from her grandmother's knee back into bed and settled again. They stayed for a moment, stroking her hair, smoothing down blankets, plumping up pillows.

'Shh, shh, it's alright now.' Her grandmother's soothing tone took effect and the child's heart stopped hammering at her throat.

'She's alright, Lillian, just a bad dream.'

Rebecca's mother had appeared at the door looking down at her child. Rebecca turned and looked at her mother.

'Come on now, leave her, she'll be alright.' The grandmother pulled Lillian by the arm but she resisted. They left her there staring at her daughter.

Rebecca found her mother strange and remote.

'Are you better now?' she asked matter-of-factly.

'Yes, Mummy.'

Lillian turned off the light and closed the door. The child was glad she didn't have to cuddle her mother. She never found solace in an embrace with her. Her mother's actions bordered on the perfunctory and Rebecca instinctively knew something was wrong with this union.

She lay still, listening as the river rhythmically beat against the rocks and the moon's rays lit up parts of the room through the open Venetian blinds. In a brief moment of silence, she could hear the lonely sound of an owl – *mow-poke, mow-poke*. She loved this house and this room; it smelt of timber and the beach. The bed was huge, the sheets were clean and starched and her grandmother always arranged pillows around her so she wouldn't fall over the side. The bedside tables were made of local pine and on them crochet doilies had been placed underneath small crystal dishes. She wasn't allowed to touch these for they contained her grandmother's jewellry; a watch, the odd necklace, a cameo ring and a few various drop earrings with blue and gold semi-precious stones. But the thing that fascinated Rebecca the most was the dimpled bottle of perfume with a leaf shaped stop. The perfume had the most wonderful scent, so sweet and light, like a breath from an exotic garden. She stretched out her hand and touched the sides of the bottle assuring herself that everything was still in place.

The radio was playing in the other room, a door slammed. Her father had arrived home from the late shift. He wouldn't come and say goodnight; it wasn't his way. He would be in an angry mood, as always.

'Don't teach the child bad habits, Harold,' Kathleen chided from somewhere else in the house. He was never able to fool her.

It was late March 1952, on a Saturday morning. It was going to be a warm day. The sun was streaming in and Rebecca was sitting on her grandfather's knee sharing toast he had dipped into his cup of tea; small droplets of melted butter were now gathering on top of the brown liquid. He was wearing his gardening clothes. A worn out, old, peaked, cloth cap sat on his head, completely covering his growing bald patch and thinning hair. It all had the effect of framing his kindly face. He secretly passed her another piece of tea-soaked toast.

'Are you going to pick gooseberries today, Grandpa?'

'Yes, love. Are you going to work in the garden with me?'

She nodded in assent. 'Where's Daddy?'

'Gone to work, love,' he replied, giving his granddaughter a reassuring pat on the hand.

His garden was a wondrous sight and it was where he spent most of his spare time. He would always pick a piece of fruit for her to try. Gooseberries were her favourite.

'I think your Aunt Pat is here,' he said, looking out the window.

Patricia Whitman was climbing the steps towards the door and Rebecca ran to open it. Patricia swooped her up and twirled her around. They giggled together.

'She's just had breakfast,' Harold called out as he sank another piece of toast.

'It's alright, Dad.' She sat her down. 'I have something for you,' she whispered to Rebecca, creating a climate of intimacy while promptly pulling a huge shell from her bag. It was the colour of sand with ridges and sharp curled-up ends. Inside was smooth and pink and part mystery as it curled away to darkness.

'Put it up to your ear, can you hear the ocean?'

Rebecca dutifully did as she was asked and listened but wasn't sure what she was hearing. She said yes anyway because she would do anything to please her beautiful, much-loved aunt with the dark brown eyes and long painted nails.

'Where's Lillian, Dad?'

'Still in bed with a headache, I think, or maybe she's gone outside.' He shook his head almost imperceptibly.

'Ces has gone down to the beach,' she mentioned casually as she sneaked a bit of his toast, licking the butter off her fingers. 'Ok if he stays for lunch?'

Cecil Newton, a New Zealander, was her latest boyfriend who had been in her life for several months. He was a head taller than Patricia, about thirty years of age with dull brown hair and a face full of disappointment. He was the only son of a wealthy sheep farming family. He'd come to Tasmania, bought up some acreage in Huonville and a small run-down dwelling at Bonnet Hill, not far from Taroona, all to prove to his doubting father he could make it on his own. He wanted to grow apples. Kath and Harry, as he annoyingly referred to Patricia's parents, had their doubts about him; they found him too brash and familiar. Added to that, he was Catholic. Despite the well-intentioned actions of kind souls, centuries of old suspicions and prejudices still remained in the hearts of a Catholic and a Church of England believer.

Patricia adored him, so they shut their mouths and hoped it would all go away. Rebecca wasn't sure about him.

'Alright with me. Ask Mum though, she's the cook. What are you wearing those for?'

'I like them, Dad,' Patricia replied in defense of her loose beige cotton trousers. She now lived independently, unusual amongst her friends (most of whom were married), earned a good wage as a typist in a law office that mainly specialised in conveyancing, had a driver's licence, her own little car and made most of her clothes. She was of strong character, fun and full of life. Her father didn't like to see women in trousers. He still preferred them in dresses, hats and gloves.

'S'pose they look alright.'

She kissed him on the top of his cap, almost skipped towards Rebecca, her white blouse filling like a sail, kissed her on the cheek and swished past, leaving behind a strong reminder of her perfume. The young child was in love with this striking image of womanhood. Patricia Whitman was the youngest of the two daughters born to Kathleen and Harold and was considered to be the beauty, by far.

The Second World War saw the demise of a number of family businesses, but Harold and Kathleen's medium-sized grocery shop in North Hobart still survived. 'Mr. Whitman is such a nice man,' was the general comment made by housewives who shopped in the area. Harold was always whistling (although he was tone deaf) while busy serving, cutting a pound of butter off a large slab or filling up a brown paper bag with an ounce of this or that and giving away a free lolly to a child, much to Kathleen's chagrin.

'We can't afford to give things away Harry,' she would say.

'It's alright, love. Brightens up their day, besides, they'll always come back, buy something else.'

She couldn't argue with his logic but still, it irked her.

They remained affluent enough to add two small rooms and continue to make minor improvements to their small, double-storey, creosote covered timber house in Shell Beach Road, Taroona, a growing suburb just a few kilometres south of Hobart. They had installed a small pond at the front and randomly planted hydrangeas, yellow and white daisies, lavender, fuchsia, and, Kathleen's favourite, a climbing yellow rose. There was no planning to any of it but it produced a balance of colour and harmony. Harold continued improving and muddling around in his already extensive vegetable and fruit garden, which was located on the higher part of the sloping land at the back of the house, on Saturdays and Sundays after church, weather permitting.

There were earth and concrete steps at intervals that led up to the top of the slope and a large flattened area, all covered in flowers. At this height, there was a clear view of the Derwent River and the tops of branches swinging in the breeze, with birds flying back and forth squabbling for position. Eating her favourite fruit and chatting in four-year-old talk with her grandfather was Rebecca's happy place – her grandfather's too. To her it was where the fairies lived and to him it was heaven, where God would like to live.

The house itself was situated at the bottom of a dirt road where the land momentarily plateaued before plummeting again towards the Derwent River. The Whitmans had been there for about four years.

Rebecca and her grandfather were immersed in their tiered wonderland when Rebecca's mother appeared quietly beside her. Rebecca didn't want her there because her presence always ended their magic time together. Something in her mother's manner always sent Rebecca into alert mode. But this time, there was a smile on her face, a funny sort of smile, not the sort of wide, opened smile like Aunty Pat, rather, a small widening of her thin lips that stopped short at the sides of a thin line.

Lillian was tall with eyes that looked black but in fact were dark brown. Her black hair was permed and eyebrows penciled. She had been ill off and on as a child and had a suffocating attachment to her mother. Kathleen and Harold knew she wasn't as talented as Pat but did their best with a puzzling daughter. She had a job working in an office in Hobart as a typist and stuck at it, but she was never really happy.

'I brought up your bucket and spade. I thought you might like a walk down to the beach.'

'Yes, Mummy,' said Rebecca, guardedly. She wasn't sure if her mother was in a good mood or not. Lillian had moments of ordinariness, and perhaps this was one of them.

'Off you go then. I'll help Grandpa with some gardening.'

'You feeling better now?' asked Harold.

'Much better, Dad.'

'You don't have to go, love. You can stay with Grandpa,' Harold assured her.

Rebecca didn't really want to leave but the spell was broken. She liked the little beach in the cove anyway, so she kissed her grandfather and left, carrying her bucket and spade, off for another adventure.

Halfway down the slope, Kathleen was waiting to take her the rest of the way. She picked her up and they slowly made their way to the back door.

'Now, darling, you walk down to the beach and Grandma will come down shortly to be with you, alright? You can have a little play before we eat.'

'I can do it by myself,' said the proud Rebecca, who often walked up and down the steep track in her search for things that mattered to her. Shells, petals of colourful flowers and pebbles to add to the pond.

'I know you can, darling, but Grandma wants to come too. I want to see your shells. Now, remember, do not go near the water.'

Sometimes it was hard not to put her feet in the water when the tide came in. At those times Rebecca quickly moved to the bits of sand that remained dry, keeping her family's warnings foremost in her mind. She never told them of her near misses.

'Alright, Grandma.' Rebecca was not in the habit of arguing with her grandparents.

Rebecca started slowly walking down the steep, dirt track passing the house located just below and next door to the Whitmans'. There was a girl who lived there too, the same age and ironically with the same name. Her family shortened it to Becky. Rebecca's family encouraged a friendship between the girls.

'Why don't you go and play with Becky? She wants to play with you,' her grandmother often asked.

'I don't like her,' answered Rebecca, looking down to avoid her grandmother's eyes. She didn't want to tell her why.

One day the girls were sitting on the wall that surrounded the pond. Neither were talking, just swishing their fingers around in the water and watching the moving fish. Becky starting picking up some tadpoles from the pond and squeezing them between her fingers, killing any hope of a future frog. Rebecca became angry and told her to stop and go away. Becky never came back and that was fine with Rebecca.

Once past Becky's house, four-year-old Rebecca looked for a treasure along the track to put in her bucket. She always felt there was something magic here in this place. Beside the track there were all sorts of wonders: ferns, pigface, lilac bells and wild berries. By the time she reached the beach, she had collected some leaves, a few coloured pebbles, a frond from a fern and a dead insect.

It was a little windy but warm on the beach. She put sand in the bucket and found a shell that pleased her. Large, ancient rocks, flattened by the water, stretched out far beyond the sand line. At low tide you could walk on them and investigate the life in puddles left behind. She saw something, a short distance away up the beach, lying on one of the black flat rocks, right where the water lapped at the edges. It was white and flapping, like a pillowslip on a clothesline. She walked towards it, curious. As she came closer, she peered at it, tentative at first. Ignoring all she had been warned, she carefully stepped over the slippery wet surface to look closer.

'Aunty Pat! Aunty Pat!' she shouted. 'What are you doing?'

There was no response. Her aunt's eyes were open and water was spilling over her feet.

'Aunty Pat, you have to come home. You will get wet.' Prodding her aunt proved useless; her body didn't move. Rebecca was transfixed; noise of the water became thunder in her ears. She noticed blood coming from her aunt's head, swilling around with the movement of the river. Rebecca ran and ran, slipping, getting up and running as fast as she could, frightened and suddenly cold.

Just as she started up the track, Kathleen was on her way down.

'Grandma, Grandma! Aunty Pat is hurt.'

'What do you mean, darling?' Kathleen happily swept her granddaughter up in her arms. She noticed she was wet and shivering.

'Have you been near the water? I told you not to do that.'

'Grandma, Aunty Pat is hurt. She's over there.'

They were now back at the end of the track and on the beach. Kathleen looked in the direction of Rebecca's little pointed finger. She lowered her granddaughter slowly.

In a voice purposely calm, she sent Rebecca to fetch Harold.

Chapter 4

The Present

'Bec, Bec, are you ok? Bec!'

Someone was shaking her awake. Her eyes opened suddenly; her husband was bending over her.

'Did you have a nightmare? You're sweating.' Andrew was concerned.

'What! Oh … sorry, I—I must have been dreaming.' She rubbed her eyes.

'Yeah, you were moaning and mumbling a lot. Are you alright? What on earth were you dreaming about?' He was standing with her morning coffee.

She was still a bit groggy and tired. 'Not sure, can't remember it all. The family were standing in a line and I was running for protection and they all just stood there waiting or something; very odd.'

Her heart was racing and it took a moment to realise she was safe and not running, she was home with her thoughtful man and a hot coffee.

'Well, as long as it wasn't about wild sex with one of my rivals.' He smiled, but his frown gave it away – he was worried.

'You don't have a rival, Andrew,' she said, and kissed him.

'You do realise it's Friday and you have to be at work in … an hour.'

'Shit, right, of course.' Gulping her coffee, she headed for the shower.

Andrew had noticed a difference in her since the event of three weeks ago. Rebecca had quiet moments and longer walks. He noticed her just sitting, thinking. Sadness appeared on her face more often. She had taken to having the odd cigarette again. He hated that.

The dog was still with them. No one came to claim it and they didn't enquire. He knew she wanted to keep it. They were trying to think of a name for it and wondered if it would confuse the dog by doing so. For the moment she responded to 'girl'. 'Come on, girl, do you want to go for a walk?' or 'Girl, do you want a biscuit?' all had the desired reaction. The little dog was happy and settled now. No one wanted to part with her.

Nothing was known about this Ms Taylor's health or progress. Police hadn't come to ask any more questions so that was that.

Driving on her way to the school Rebecca was in the between moment of still feeling the effects of an awful dream, now hardly remembered, and reality. By the time she reached school, all was calm within her and she braced herself for the busy time that was the end of term.

She entered the small administration office of the primary school; The atmosphere was bordering on chaotic. Phones ringing, parents and teaching staff alike asking questions, requesting things and it all had to be done now. The bursar was red in the face and flustered but that was end of term as usual.

During the day Andrew called to give Rebecca the news. He had secured a contract to design a small office complex in the township. He was over the moon and she was delighted for him. Celebrations were promised for the evening and Mark was coming over with a friend. Perhaps they could go out for dinner?

'Good idea, I'll book somewhere,' said Andrew.

Everything was working out and Rebecca took a deep breath and smiled broadly for the first time in a while.

'Hey, Bec!' Her favourite colleague Jean beckoned her over to a quieter spot in the office.

Rebecca gave her the good news.

'Wow, that's fantastic,' she said and gave her a big unabashed hug. 'I've been worried about you; you haven't been yourself. Anyway, it's obviously all good now.'

'Yes, it is.' Rebecca smiled.

'This is probably nothing, Bec, but someone rang for you yesterday. She had a strange voice actually. She asked if you worked here. I asked for her name and details for a return call but she hung up. I couldn't say you don't work here. Should I have?'

'Please, Jean, it's fine. That would be my mother. She knows I don't take calls from her at work. Andrew must have given her the number. He should know better.' She gave Jean a pat on the arm. 'It's all good, not a problem. Frankly, my mother and her issues would fill a psychiatric conference for a week.'

Jean thought she was joking.

When she arrived home the champagne was already flowing. Mark had arrived with a gorgeous-looking woman and Andrew was beaming with joy. He kissed his wife with passion, nuzzled into her neck and spoke, out of hearing, of love and sex in her ear.

'Are you happy because of the job or the gorgeous girl?' she whispered.

'Ha! Ha!' said Andrew.

Mark and his friend looked on at these two with wide smiles.

Dinner was perfect – a lot of wine and laughter flowed. Mark was showing Rebecca more attention and sympathy.

'Did you give Mum my work number?' she asked Andrew, by the by.

'I haven't spoken to your mother in ages, and even if I did, I know the rules.'

'Oh … that's strange.'

The query was quickly dismissed, the fun and laugher kept on. It was one of the happiest times in quite a while, for all of them.

Rebecca and Andrew made love that night – it was reminiscent of their first time. They slept the sleep of lovers and Rebecca felt at peace.

Chapter 5

The Past

Harold, Lillian and Rebecca returned to the beach. Kathleen was still standing in the same position, staring, unable to move. A few people had gathered and a man went over to inspect Pat's body. He confirmed she was dead. Everyone was shocked. Rebecca started to cry and put her head into her mother's stiff body. Lillian was riveted to the scene and made no attempt to comfort her child. Kathleen lifted Rebecca to her breast. It was the only movement she made. People talked quietly, if they talked at all.

There was a newly opened small milk bar and paper shop not far away. Harold ran up the track and took off in his Hillman to ring for police.

After what seemed like a long time the police finally arrived. An ambulance waited at the top of the walking track. Two ambulance men came walking down with a canvas stretcher between them. Police moved people away and the family just waited. With her body covered, Pat was taken away to the morgue.

The family went back up the track to the house. Harold carried Rebecca whose world was shattered. She was hysterical and angry. Why did her aunt die? Why did she do that? She couldn't comprehend anything. She hated the walking track, she hated the beach, she hated the house, she hated everything. She ran to the big bed when they arrived at the house and buried her face in the soft white pillows. It took ages to console her until she finally slept from exhaustion.

The rest of the family gathered in the kitchen and police came to ask questions. They had inspected the whole area where Pat had died but found nothing. Their shoes and bottoms of their trousers were wet through and Kathleen found the strength to offer towels and cups of tea. Lillian finally moved to help. She had barely spoken.

Harold told them all he knew from breakfast time that morning to now. How happy she was, how she had gone down to the beach to meet Cecil. He described her life, her work and the people she worked with as far as he knew. He gave them her address and a key with permission to search it all. They particularly wanted to interview Cecil. Details of his address were also given. After consoling words and promises to find out how this happened, they left.

For a moment there was silence, then Kathleen and Harold held each other and cried. Their beautiful daughter was gone and they were inconsolable. Lillian sat across from them, her face crumpled now and tears running down her face. They grabbed her hand and for the first time in many years they were all one in their despair.

Rebecca's father, John, was yet to arrive home from work. They would have to go through the events all over again.

Next morning, it was decided Harold and Kathleen would take Rebecca with them while they visited some extended family members to tell them what had happened. It was better than finding out from the newspaper. Harold had a niece, Marjorie. She and her husband Jack had two children a bit older than Rebecca … It would do her good to be with them, wouldn't it? She had hardly said a word and barely eaten. Every now and then a sob would escape – it sounded like a hiccup. Her grandparents felt they were living in a nightmare and did everything by rote. Responsibility of Rebecca was the only thing that kept them from sinking.

While they were alone John questioned his wife.

'Did you do anything to her?' John Parke asked.

'What! No! Of course I didn't.' Lillian was red-eyed and bedraggled in appearance. She hadn't slept well.

'You were always jealous of her.'

'So, what of it?'

'Tell me everything that happened.'

'I had a quick talk with Cecil before he started down the track.'

'What sort of talk?'

'Well … you know. How are you, Cecil? Nice day, roast will be ready soon, something like that. I can't remember it all.'

'Then?'

'Pat passed me on her way down the beach to meet up with Cecil. They were going to have a little walk before we all sat down to eat, that's all.'

'Were you with them?'

'No, I went up to the garden with Dad. I'm tired, John, my head is aching. I need a Vincent powder.'

He prepared some water and a cup of tea for her. He didn't know what to think about all this. They were waiting for a rental house to become available. John was a low-income earner. His work varied from working on the ferry to washing dishes and other odd jobs. Lillian's parents would help them financially as best they could but they were always deeply worried about their financial situation.

The couple met through a miscellaneous wants ad in the *Mercury*. Kathleen and Harold wanted something completely different for their older daughter, someone who would understand her strange ways and accept her for it. Their wedding took place under financial restraint, as a small affair. Lillian didn't wear a traditional wedding dress, there were no attendants and sandwiches and cakes were provided by Kathleen and Harold's family. All tried to be happy and make the best of it. Her parents still questioned why she did it.

Rebecca seemed like an angel from heaven when she arrived after an easy birth. They couldn't believe how perfect she was. Lillian had days when she couldn't cope and Kathleen stepped in. It was inevitable a bond would arise between granddaughter and grandmother.

John was desperate to get out of the situation. He didn't dislike Lillian's family. Actually, he was ambivalent about them, but this was not where he wanted to be and, as far as he was concerned, they'd been there long enough. Having been brought up in a series of foster homes, constantly running away and wagging school meant he had no close relationships. Lillian's family would be no loss to him. Besides, he'd just been hired, gaining a permanent job at the

Mercury loading papers ready for delivery and any other jobs he was capable of doing. He was to start in two weeks. As soon as a place was available, they could leave.

Rebecca and her grandparents arrived back after tea, obviously drained. Little Rebecca briefly kissed her parents and was put to bed. The adults sat around the dining table. Things had to be organised. Pat's body would not be released until a post-mortem was conducted so funeral arrangements were put on hold. Harold would go back and open the shop – much had to be done. He would ask other family to help out with serving customers; he couldn't yet face them himself. Kathleen and Lillian would stay at home and do what had to be done. John would go back to work – for now.

Over the next few days there were visitors from far and wide bringing flowers, sympathy and help wherever needed. Kathleen had many brothers and sisters, some of whom Rebecca had never seen. At times Lillian took her daughter for a walk up to the garden, seemingly to shield her daughter from conversations about Pat's death. Rebecca didn't mind. She didn't really want to talk to the aunts and uncles, she was too sad. Besides, she was enjoying her mother's unusually kind attention.

The police came to visit again and Lillian was now questioned. She gave them details of her actions that day. They were interested in anything to do with Cecil. His house was still intact although it looked like some clothing was missing. No personal identity papers were found either; he was gone. An alert was issued by police – he was considered a person of interest and missing. If he was sighted, they wanted to know about it straight away. An article about the incident was posted in the *Mercury* along with a photo of Cecil.

Two weeks went by before they received the coroner's report on a Monday, delivered by special mail, sooner than they expected. It was detailed but the family focused on the most important parts. Pat was not sexually assaulted; she had been hit with force to her face and chest, resulting in some bruising. The coroner concluded this force most probably resulted in her falling onto the rocks, hitting her head, causing damage to her skull. Her body had been released to the funeral parlour. Rebecca, who was playing outside, didn't hear any of these details.

Pat's funeral was arranged for the following Saturday at St Stephen's Anglican Church, Sandy Bay Road. Funeral notices were posted in the paper. It was short notice but the church was very obliging and relatives would drop everything to be there and support each other. The grocery shop closed for a few days.

This was a day the family dreaded. At the same time they felt it had to be done as soon as possible. Somehow they knew that after she was buried, and things quietened down, they would finally be able to properly mourn her.

On that sombre Saturday, people slowly entered the church, were greeted and handed a program of the service. Most wore black and talked in hushed tones. All the extended family was there. Friends of Pat from her sporting days and all the colleagues she had worked with also attended, as did many customers from the grocery shop. The church was full.

Harold, Kathleen, Lillian, John and Rebecca sat at the front. The open coffin had been placed at the front near the altar. Hymns were sung, people prayed and the minister said kind words about the lovely and talented Patricia Whitman.

'Now,' said the minister, 'there is someone here today who wants to say a special goodbye.'

Harold stood up with his granddaughter and approached the coffin. The organist was softly playing 'Abide With Me' written by Henry Francis Lyte. He lifted Rebecca so she was able to see her aunt who was dressed in her favourite blue. Pat looked peaceful and beautiful. Some makeup had been applied to her face and light pink lipstick to her perfectly shaped mouth.

Rebecca placed her precious bucket and spade beside her aunt, along with some pebbles, flower petals, a bird's feather and the large shell Pat had given her. She had insisted on doing this and nothing was going to stop her. With her four-year-old logic she was sure Aunty Pat would show God these things, ask him to put the shell to his ear and see if he could hear the ocean. They can talk about it, she reasoned to her grandparents.

Before lifting her down, Rebecca patted her aunt's dress and made sure all the gifts from her were in place.

'Goodbye, Aunty Pat,' she said.

They slowly walked back to their seats where Harold comforted his grieving wife and John held a tearful Lillian. The minister had never witnessed such reverence from a child of that age.

There was quiet sobbing from the women and their usually stoic men were wiping away tears from their faces. They had witnessed something that would stay in their minds for a very long time.

Chapter 6

The Present

It was one of those mornings unusual for winter: mild, no wind and full sunshine. Andrew was up first but only just. Rebecca, smelling toast and coffee, came quietly up behind him. They kissed, a long kiss, both still luxuriating in the intimate sex-filled atmosphere of the night before.

'Are you going off to the office?' she asked.

'Not if I can help it. I have enough to be able to work from home today.'

She was pleased for a change. Normally she liked to be by herself. Their dog came pattering into the kitchen. Having finally decided to keep her, in the absence of any news from her previous owner, they decided to make her their own and named her Meg, or Meggy if they wanted to indulge in baby speak. She came either way, happy and wagging her short white tail. They loved her.

After eating and showering they settled to their own particular tasks for the day. As Rebecca was on school holidays, hers wasn't as pressing. A grade six English teacher asked if she would be happy to mark some of the students work. The particular teacher would look at the papers again but, 'It would be of tremendous help to have another pair of eyes'. She was aware of Rebecca's experience.

The grade six students had been reading a variety of books and were encouraged to write one page about the one they really enjoyed and why. They were marked on their grammar, spelling and comprehension. At the bottom of the page, they were asked to find a noun and pronoun and write them down as well. *Good stuff*, thought Rebecca.

Andrew was busy making a series of phone calls. Another happy, relaxed day at the house of Amos'.

With the marking of the grade six compositions finished, Rebecca had an urge to look up her grandmother's family history. Her time was free, holiday time, why not? She had recently joined a genealogical society site that prompted her to bring out a box of old photos and spend the afternoon researching. Something she didn't know: her grandmother was born in Nerrina, Victoria. Well! That was a revelation. She had ten siblings. Two girls had died, one at a few months old, the other not lasting beyond a year. And there were twin boys, one of whom didn't survive beyond two years of age. Tears welled up.

She looked up Kathleen's parents. They were married in 1887 in Nerrina. One of their children was born in Footscray, but the rest were listed as being born in Bungaree and Little Bendigo. Something long forgotten came to mind. Kathleen had talked about the gold rush times in casual conversations with her brother when he came to visit. Rebecca only remembered three of Kathleen's siblings, two great aunts and a great uncle. Her grandmother was always happy and laughing when they were around. She'd seen them before, long ago, but the box of old photos now became more important and some rummaging among them provided an old black and white of Kathleen. Rebecca had forgotten how attractive she looked in her ruffled collar, large hat and long white dress. The resemblance to Pat was unmistakable. If only they'd talked together about her grandmother's background. Another older and smaller box was retrieved. She opened it. Under a sweet-smelling scarf, black beret, a bracelet and a funeral program was a photo of Pat. She compared the two. There was no mistaking it. Pat resembled her mother.

Kathleen had worked hard. It was before the time-saving appliances of today. All bed linen and clothes were put in the copper for boiling, then through the wringer by hand and hung out to dry. There was the shop, preparing meals, endless household chores. Rebecca, once too young to understand, now asked the question, *How did she manage it all? On top of that, she had to deal with Mum. I could never thank them enough for what they did for me.*

'For God's sake, stop wallowing,' she admonished herself. The boxes were carefully put away. She went to make coffee.

Chapter 7

The Past

Sometimes luck favours nefarious men.

Cecil knew she was dead; he just knew it. Panic gripped him like a vice. He couldn't breathe. Suddenly, his legs were propelling him towards the track – he must get out of here now!

He caught sight of Rebecca walking down towards the beach. She was distracted, looking at flowers, smelling them, picking them off and putting them into her bucket. He dived into the bushes until she passed. Scrambling up the hill through the undergrowth on hands and knees, he reached his car. He had parked just to the right of the track on the side of the road under a tree. Keeping low, he opened the door and slid into the driver's seat. No one saw him, he was sure. His car was always reliable and it started immediately. Slowly, so not to attract attention, he drove up the hill. Shell Beach Road was U-shaped. He was now situated on the other side of it, away from the track and the house. He reached the main road, turned left and headed for Bonnet Hill, five minutes away.

He grabbed what he could from the house. Some clothes, personal papers and, most importantly, a small case containing a large amount of cash he had hidden under the floorboards. He quickly took off his expensive suit and waistcoat, jammed them into his case, put on some old clothes and a cap, lowered as far as possible over his eyes. He ran to the car and drove to Hobart, arriving in fifteen minutes. He abandoned the car in a side street and walked to the wharf. His idea was to ask for a berth on a fishing boat, any boat; he didn't care where it was going, as long as it was out of Hobart. After asking a fisherman he discovered no one else was going out today.

'But, there's a couple of boats taking off for the Antarctic over there, if you're looking for a journey. They're stopping at New Zealand first though. Bloody idiots, if you ask me,' the fisherman said, cigarette hanging from his mouth. He turned back to his nets, not thinking for a moment that the man in the cap would take the suggestion seriously. The fisherman was going tomorrow himself, back to Port Phillip Bay. Fishing was better there he was told and he wanted to prepare himself and his boat for the grueling journey across Bass Strait. The encounter with the scraggy man was quickly dismissed from his mind.

Cecil, still holding his cap low over his face, ran as fast as he could to boats docked at Princes Wharf and asked for the captain of the smaller vessel. Trying his best not to seem desperate, he asked if it were possible for him to go with them as far as New Zealand. He spun a story of a dying father and his fear of flight in getting there. He could pay in cash. There was some hesitancy by the Norwegian captain. This was an international group of scientists going to the South Pole who had gained financial support from their governments for the expedition. He didn't want to jeopardise it by taking on a stranger. After a few moments of gentle persuasion and appealing to the captain's sense of decency, the captain agreed. They had to call into New Zealand anyway to pick up another scientist. Where was the harm? He would put the cash to good use, maybe towards the purchase of Huskies, if they were needed.

He took Cecil down below and showed him to a spare bunk. They were leaving in an hour. He was welcome to come and eat with them when they were on their way.

Cecil couldn't believe his good fortune. Considering his lack of morality he knew, deep down, he didn't deserve it but now, he could breathe and feel safe. There was planning and thinking to be done – he had bought some much-needed time. First, he would change his name while on board. It would be Taylor, Norman Taylor.

Chapter 8

After Patricia's funeral, the coffin was driven away to Cornelian Bay Cemetery. Only the men were in the car that followed – Harold, John, Harold's brother and a brother of Kathleen's. Kathleen and Lillian couldn't face it. They and other family would visit the grave often over time, but not now.

The small funeral procession curved its way from the church up the main road. Most of the time the Derwent River was visible and Harold broke down on seeing it glistening in the sun. The minister was present at the cemetery. He said some words of prayer. The coffin was slowly lowered and the men walked gradually away holding on to Harold tightly so he wouldn't fall while weakened with grief.

Everyone, including neighbors, was invited back to Harold and Kathleen's house. No one had ever observed so many vehicles parked there in one day. They wound right up to the top and back down the other side of the U-shaped road.

All the women brought cakes or sandwiches or both. Some looked after the tea and biscuits. Even though Harold was a non-drinker and certainly not an advocate of alcohol, sweet or dry sherry was permitted and he was the one that offered it around the throng, despite his shaking hands. John helped in the kitchen, washing up while talking to some of the men who joined him there.

Children were amongst the guests and Rebecca was encouraged to play with them but she didn't want to. There wasn't a time when someone or other held her hand or lifted her up and remarked how pretty she was with her large blue eyes and olive skin. Someone said, 'Oh, look, she has a double crown.' She didn't know what that meant. At that moment, she just wanted to be left alone. She snuck off to her favourite place, the large bed, and eventually went to sleep.

Kathleen and Lillian weren't required to do anything, for which they were grateful because they were weary. They sat together at the dining table and talked to anyone who wanted to have a conversation. Of course, no matter how delicately it was approached the question would inevitably be raised. 'Do you know how it happened? Who did it? Who do the police suspect? What a terrible, terrible thing.' Some men offered to thoroughly bash the person themselves, break their bones. Kathleen proffered what information she had. Lillian remained silent; at times, she just hung her head.

Eventually, people started to leave. Every one of them offered their help in whatever way and whenever it was needed. The family was dear to many and they all felt helpless in not being able to remedy it for them.

The four of them sat around the table for a while talking about how to proceed. They would collect Pat's things from her flat, decide what to do with her clothes, her car, her jewellery. Of course, there were some things they would never part with. Rebecca would also be given a chance to pick something of her aunt's belongings. All photos would stay with the family. For now, they decided to go to bed and try to sleep. Rebecca hadn't stirred. It had been a habit to let her go to sleep in her grandparent's bed then move her to the smaller bedroom without waking her. Tonight, they decided to leave her where she lay. They would spread out to the smaller rooms and the couch.

Tears still trickled down cheeks without warning, eyes were swollen, hearts were broken and they didn't see how they were ever going to recover from this tragedy.

Chapter 9

As promised, the vessel carrying scientists and equipment for the Antarctic exhibition left Princes Wharf an hour after Cecil embarked. The larger boat was leaving the next day and going straight to the South Pole. Scientists from both vessels would meet at Maudheim in Antarctica, a place Cecil had never heard of and had no interest in.

The calm waters of the Derwent River, along with the sounds of men's voices and the diesel engine, comforted him. Extreme fatigue won over fear and guilt; he was soon asleep. After a few hours the thud of the boat slamming into the waves woke him. Cecil had forgotten where he was. What was the time? He suddenly felt very sick. He grabbed a nearby bucket and vomited violently. His head and heart were pounding. Everything came back to him. He vomited again. He lay down but the boat kept rocking, rising, falling, rolling, tipping him against the wall then to the floor. Holding on to a steel upright that was supporting the bunks, he lay down again but didn't let go. He closed his eyes; nausea was ever-present. Someone was shaking him.

'Sorry, you feel sick, ja?'

'Yes, very,' said Cecil.

'Many men sick on boat now, ja?' This was a statement from the wide smiling Swedish man, not a question.

'I don't know, can't get up. What time is it?'

'Is, what you say … um …' He scratched his head. 'Hundra timmar … is nineteen hundred hours.'

'Seven o'clock, right, thank you.'

'I will get you something to eat.' Holding on to anything to keep his footing, the smiling Swedish man disappeared up a ladder.

Cecil's first trip to Tasmania had been on a flying boat from Auckland to Sydney. From there he had travelled by train to Melbourne, once changing trains at Albury due to the difference in gauges. After a day of rest, he'd booked a cabin on the Taroona, ironically the place name of the area he would make his home.

While in Launceston, he searched for a car to buy and settled on a second-hand green Morris Minor that was advertised in the local paper. It was nearly new and in good condition. The next day, following directions from local inhabitants and checking his map, he travelled down the Midland Highway to Hobart. He spent some time there, visited the library, researching anything about Huonville and surrounds, something he'd started looking into while in New Zealand. He visited an estate agent and (from many discussions and much paperwork) acquired some acreage in Huonville containing an apple orchard. He had to learn how to maintain it. Then he bought a small timber residence, partially furnished, in Bonnet Hill. Bonnet Hill had a small population and neighbours were spaced far away from each other. All this had suited the young Cecil very well. He had been excited and eager to prove his worth.

The Swedish man came back with some salty biscuits and a cup of clear soup.

'You eat some, ja,' he said, still smiling.

'Thank you, I'll try,' Cecil replied, feeling very weak. He vowed his next voyage, if there were to be one, would be by plane.

Two days later he felt much better and went up top to join the party of scientists and crew. The Tasman Sea had calmed to smooth waters and a slight breeze. He thanked the Swedish man for looking after him.

There was an Englishman on board and Cecil was able to have a conversation. He hadn't shaved and still wore his cap and the same clothes. He knew he must have looked skinny, grimy and red-eyed, but he wanted to. The less like Cecil Newton the better. He deftly avoided all the usual questions – where he live and where he worked – by steering the conversation to where this Englishman was going and the research he and the team would be studying.

After five days the boat arrived at Port Chalmers Wharf, New Zealand at ten am. He shook hands, said a grateful thank you to all and disembarked. He stood on the wharf, taking a moment for his land legs to work; he was still shaky.

Standing beside him was a man doubled over with equipment on his back and bags all around his feet. He was waiting to embark. After a few words they started talking. Cecil asked about accommodation in the area.

'Funny you should ask that,' said the New Zealand scientist. 'My house is vacant, the person who was going to rent it, well, didn't.'

'Is that right?' replied Cecil, now very interested.

'I tell you what. How about I get my gear on board and I can take you to it? They're going to be a couple of hours getting more supplies,' he said, pointing towards the boat. 'The cottage is only a few minutes up the hill, you can have a look.'

'Yes, I'm interested,' said Cecil, hiding his eagerness.

After waiting half an hour, the man reappeared. He helped Cecil with his bags and they walked to Mark Street. On their way they introduced themselves. The scientist was Edward Martin and Cecil provided his alias, Norman Taylor.

The old small cottage had beautiful views, was small, warm, inviting and clean. It had a telephone, a refrigerator, heating, a washing machine, a bath and a small but ample electric stove.

The amount of rent was settled and Cecil paid him eight months in advance, in cash. He also agreed to pay electricity and telephone bills. He could do this at the post office. In addition, Cecil was given the keys to a small van he could use. Regular use would prevent the battery going flat. If Cecil vacated before Martin was due back, keys and any monies owed would be hidden in a place agreed by both.

They shook hands and Cecil was alone. His emotions were still in turmoil, guilt was always present, but this had turned out better than he had hoped. And he was close to the wharf – if he had to, he could make another quick exit. Plenty of time to think of the next step.

He finally took off his cap. He felt lucky.

Chapter 10

Two months had past and Kathleen and Harold had made a decision. They would sell the house. Leaving it and Taroona would be devastating in itself but staying near the place where Patricia had met her death was even more so. Rebecca hadn't been down the track since, preferring to spend her time in her grandpa's garden.

'Would you like me to take you down, love?' he would ask her.

'No, thank you, Grandpa,' she would reply.

They worried about her; she had brightened up a little but it was obvious she was not the same happy child.

The police had made another visit. They had investigated every mode used for a getaway. Trains, Cambridge Airport, trams, taxis, and the wharfs. They showed a copy of Cecil's photo. Nothing. They also extended their investigation to the Royal Hobart and Calvary hospitals. Another item was inserted in the *Mercury* along with his photo. This yielded nothing. They could only conclude he may have met with foul play and therefore be lying injured or dead.

'We are looking into one of our officers visiting New Zealand to talk to his father. We have discovered he still lives in an old property on a sheep farm located at North Island. We will exhaust every avenue,' they said. They repeated their condolences and left.

All Patricia's affairs had been arranged. As Patricia died interstate, it was legally decided her parents would inherit her estate. There were just a few pounds in her bank account so the family agreed to start a bank account for Rebecca with the amount. Some of her clothes went to other family and friends after Lillian chose some pieces for herself. John wanted to buy her car. He organised a small deposit and said he would give them a weekly payment until it was paid off. They agreed to the arrangement despite some misgivings.

They were not enamored with John.

Lillian had a licence but never drove. Harold and Kathleen took her to and from her work every day on their way to the grocery shop. When the buses started a service, she was happy to use them. For the rest of her life, she preferred public transport or taxis.

Rebecca was given a choice of some of her aunt Pat's belongings. She brought a little box to the table and, sitting next to her grandparents, she carefully went through all the items. After much consideration she chose a bracelet, a black beret, a scarf, which still held the smell of her aunt's perfume, a lovely photo showing her bright smile and a copy of the program of the funeral service. She loved what she had chosen and would keep them in her own safe place.

John and Lillian had secured a house for rent on Augusta Road in Lenah Valley, just north of Hobart. They would leave Taroona in a few days.

Rebecca was quiet and sad again and either spent her days in the garden or packing her things for the move. She cried to herself. Leaving her grandparents was as sad as Aunty Pat dying. When either Kathleen or Harold was near, they held her and promised they would see her, a lot. She gave them a sad smile.

By the end of the third month after Patricia's death, they had all left. Harold and Kathleen moved to a house in North Hobart. It was only two streets away from the grocery shop. Although it was nothing like Taroona, its proximity made running the grocery business easier.

Lillian, John and Rebecca also settled into their house. There was no garden to speak of around the whole house. Just grass and some trees. But there was a long verandah with steps down to the lawn, which Rebecca liked. John went to work every day and Lillian would constantly visit a friend (some strange woman she used to work with), a great aunt or members of the church. There still weren't any children to play with. Rebecca was dragged from one visit to another and made to amuse herself while the adults talked. With the exception of the aunt, all of these people were strangers to her.

By now, phones were prevalent in most households and Lillian embraced it with a manic obsession, talking for hours, sometimes in hushed tones. She also used it as a vehicle for spite. Irrational jealousy motivated a call to her parents, a family member, or an acquaintance in the small hours of the morning. Without a word she would immediately hang up.

Her little girl was left to amuse herself; she became used to it, preferred it. She played with her plastic tea set, her dolls, her teddy bear, or looked at the colourful pages of her Golden books, saying out loud the words her grandmother had taught her. She would repeat the alphabet and numbers. All a panacea for coping with a bleak household. It was better than engagement with her mother, who was becoming increasingly detached and, because of shift work, her father was rarely seen.

Kathleen and Harold called as often as they could, primarily to see how Rebecca was faring. They always picked her up, kissed her all over her face and hugged her tight. They could sense their granddaughter had lost her joyful temperament. She looked pale and tired. One of them would carry her around while talking to Lillian and John, if he were about. It was the best time when her grandparents were holding her. She went from silent to talkative and her smile would now and then appear.

She would never tell them her mother smacked her sometimes, saying she was a very naughty girl, even though she had done nothing wrong. Neither would she tell them of the day her father had smacked her bottom hard, after Lillian said she needed it for being naughty again. On that day, Rebecca screamed and wet her pants. She became frightened and lost her confidence.

For now though, she was being held by her grandparents and felt protected.

Chapter 11

Cecil had slept for twelve hours; it was morning. His first thought was to buy food and supplies. He looked at himself in a mirror on the wall in the bathroom. His beard was starting to grow, as was his hair. For the moment, he would leave it this way. He washed, dressed in old clothes and donned the old cap in its usual place, well over his eyes. Satisfied with his disguise he went exploring the local area.

After two hours he came back with plenty of produce, toiletries and a local paper. He was pleased to find there was a milk bar not far from his residence.

There was a radio in the house that sat on the kitchen bench; he turned it on. The clearest broadcast was from the New Zealand Broadcasting Service. He quickly worked out the electric stove and cooked. With eggs, bacon and bread on the table, he ate, listened and read the paper.

He was looking for work and found an advertisement wanting shearers for a sheep station, located on the southern slopes of Lake Wakatipu, commencing in October. He was an experienced shearer, gaining the skill while working on his father's sheep station. Although his body wasn't as tough after a long absence, he was sure he could do it. He rang the telephone number. After a while it was answered. Cecil made enquiries and provided his details. Apart from the truth about his skills, everything else was a lie, including the place where he gained them. The person at the other end seemed not to worry much about details; he just wanted an experienced worker who would pay his own way to the sheep station.

For now, Cecil had to occupy himself for a few months. He still had plenty of money and he was frugal – he would be alright for now. He didn't know or care about what would happen to the property he left behind. He hadn't paid much down on it anyway. In the interim he made himself busy. He cleaned walls of the house, tidied up outside, drove the small van down to Dunedin, had a look around. He purchased some books and read the papers, studied maps of the South Island, all the time keeping his head down.

It was early October 1952 when Cecil locked up the house in Port Chalmers and caught a train to Dunedin arriving later in the morning.

With the exception of a pair of moccasins, all his shearing clothes had been left behind at his father's house, so he purchased a pair of dungarees and a shearer's singlet. He had everything else he needed including a sleeping blanket.

After spending the night in Dunedin, he caught a bus to Queenstown early the next morning. Queenstown was about one hundred and eighty four miles away and the trip was going to take about five to six hours. He settled into a seat at the rear of the bus and pulled down his cap. His beard and hair had grown and he sported a moustache. No one would recognise Cecil now. The only risk was if any of the shearers at the sheep station ever worked on his father's farm on the North Island. He doubted it.

His reason for work was not a monetary one. He wanted a diversion; he wanted to work so hard he would be too tired to think. He wanted to remain hidden.

Chapter 12

A few months had passed. Harold and Kathleen worked hard in the grocery shop. Hard work helped them cope with the agony of their loss. The Whitmans remained stoic and were buoyed by family and loyal customers. Sometimes, some would quietly ask if there was any news of who had done this to their daughter. 'No, we've heard nothing,' Harold would say. People would tsk, tsk and shake their heads in dismay.

The business was steadily growing so Harold decided to engage more staff. One of Kathleen's nephews, Hector, who had previously worked there sometimes after school, was very keen. He was reliable, eager to learn, and loved working with his aunt and uncle. He was a year older than his cousin Lillian and, although they saw each other at family events, they were not close.

In October, the police came to see them at the shop. Hector took charge of the counter while Harold and Kathleen guided the police to the back of the building. The room at the rear had a table and chairs sitting beside shelves of various stock. There was a sink with some crockery and a kettle. Kathleen offered them a cup of tea, which they gratefully accepted. The sergeants (one of them a senior) opened their folders and began to talk them through everything they had actioned in their search for the person of interest, the missing Cecil Newton.

The report was detailed and thorough. They had again investigated every avenue of escape he may have used to get out of the state or, indeed, out of the country. His residence had been forensically examined, as was the surrounding area. Neighbours had been interviewed several times. No one had seen him coming or going. They discovered an abandoned green Morris Minor in a side street in Hobart that they confirmed belonged to Mr Newton. It was as though he had disappeared into thin air. They had also engaged the New Zealand police to find and interview his father.

'The police in New Zealand did locate his father,' stated the older sergeant. 'He lives in a small house by himself in Auckland. His wife died some years ago. Apparently, he sold his entire sheep station and gave his son about three quarters of the money in cash.'

Eyebrows were raised along with intakes of breath.

'How much?' asked Harold.

'Around seventy thousand pounds.'

There was a momentary silence.

'The father didn't get on with his son,' said the sergeant.

'Why give him so much money then?' asked Harold.

'Well, apparently, he wanted his son to go off and make a man of himself, as he put it. He also revealed he had never felt much for him, called him a bit soft. There were no other children and the police were under the impression he hadn't seen or ever wanted to see Cecil again,' said the other sergeant. 'They told us he didn't look very well either. He complained of constant headaches and was taking tablets.'

'It seems you won't find him then,' said Harold, despondently. 'It's hopeless.'

Kathleen looked tearful.

The sergeants were sympathetic for this family. 'We have to wind down this investigation, we don't have the manpower but we won't forget it, it will remain an open case. One day we will find him.'

All were sure it was Cecil who had killed Pat. His immediate disappearance from the scene confirmed it. It was the why that distressed them so much.

Sergeant Richard Williams and Senior Sergeant Michael Thomas rose from their seats, shook hands with Harold, nodded respectfully to Kathleen, walked to the front of the shop and left. There was nothing else they could provide.

Chapter 13

Cecil arrived at the shores of Lake Wakatipu mid afternoon that day. It had been a tiring journey. Some parts of the road were bumpy and there were a few stops to open and shut gates of farming properties.

After alighting from the bus and stretching his legs, he looked around him. Despite his tired and anxious mind, he drew a deep breath at the beautiful sight of the lake. It was surrounded by hundreds of pine trees and snow-capped mountains. The lake was blue, smooth and perfectly calm. If only he could lie on it and float away.

It was a short walk from the bus to the wharf where the TSS Earnslaw steam ship picked up passengers for a forty-five-minute trip to the shore on the other side. Cecil appreciated this peaceful time and took in the views and the fresh air.

On arrival, he stepped off the ship and walked along the jetty to meet a man at the prearranged time.

A tall, rugged and deeply sun-tanned man came walking towards him, hand extended.

'G'day, Norman Taylor?' he asked.

Cecil nearly said, 'No it's Ce—'

Shaking the man's strong grip, he said, 'Yes, hello, and you are?'

'Larry, Larry Evans. How was your trip?'

'Alright, thanks, takes a while to get here but worth it. Pretty good place.' His heart was still thumping from his near giveaway.

'You live in Port Chalmers, right?'

'At the moment. I like to move around though, see more of the place. Haven't felt the need to settle anywhere yet.'

'Yeah, well, shearing can do that to ya.'

'I hear an Australian accent. Where are you from?' said Cecil, trying to divert the conversation from himself.

'Western Australia. Too hot for me, had enough of shearing there, wanted somewhere cooler. You're a New Zealander. Where did you say you have been shearing?'

'All over,' replied Cecil, heart in his throat. He wanted an end to this questioning.

They finally reached the top of the hill. On the flat acreage stood the buildings of the Abboran Sheep Station. There were large flocks of sheep spread out in pens, ready for shearing, and covered sheds in case of rain. Wet wool couldn't be shorn. Huntaway sheepdogs sat or stood near the pens, just in case one of the flock tried to make a break for it. These dogs were revered by farmers for their hard work and intelligence. They were a station owner's most valued asset and treated accordingly.

The main house was at a distance to the right. On his left stood the shearing shed; further along were the shearers' quarters, which included a kitchen. In another shed there were two toilets, a small shower block and a washhouse. Although built as one long building, it had separate doors to rooms that housed two bunks each. Washbasins and hooks for hanging work clothes were outside each door. Its timber was weathered and white paint on the doors was peeling off in large patches. A corrugated roof completed the structure.

As they drew nearer, Cecil could hear the noise that was unique to a shearing shed.

'Hard at it then?'

'Yep,' Larry confirmed.

'What powers all this?' asked Cecil, genuinely interested.

'Diesel generators. You'll have power for shearing and enough power for the quarters but it will turn off about eight pm. I'll give you a kerosene lantern as well, just in case you need to get up for a piss or whatever,' he said with a grin. 'Showers stay hot 'til then too. Anyway, here we are, you'll have the room to yourself. Tea is served at six down there.' He pointed in the direction of the dining area. 'You've got some time to settle in now, so do that then have a look around if you want. See you at six and you can meet the other shearers.'

The room Cecil was to sleep in for the next week or two was comfortable enough. He took the lower bunk. Sheets and blankets were provided but he preferred his sleeping bag so he rolled it out on top. There was also a table and two chairs as well as a cupboard and a shelf for clothing and other items. On the back wall there was a picture of some woman in the nude. He took it down and folded it away for the next person. Pictures of nude women were of no interest to him. Images like these never evoked fantasies of sexual pleasure for Cecil; instead he found them demeaning and confronting. Not that he divulged these feelings to other men.

After arranging his things, he stepped outside to think and consider what conversations might take place with the other men. He must be on guard, non-committal, evasive, ready to lie, remember his story and his new name.

He had a quick look inside the shearing shed. Panic came back again. He hadn't done any shearing for a while, longer than he told Larry. *Calm down*, he thought. *You can do it. You have to.*

At six pm on the dot, Cecil, still wearing his cap, walked to the kitchen. He opened the door to find a room warmed by an open fire, men sitting around a dining table, and an older woman over a wood fired oven.

Larry stood up and beckoned Cecil. 'Alright, everyone.' Silence from the men. 'This is the shearer for the next couple of weeks, Norman Taylor.'

There was a 'Kia Ora' from the shearers who stood up and shook hands with the new arrival.

'This is Henry, James and Jacob,' said Larry.

'Kia Ora,' replied Cecil, repeating the New Zealand traditional hello.

Everyone sat down and the cook put a large casserole dish on the table. It was a lamb stew with vegetables accompanied by a loaf of bread that had been made on the premises. Everyone tucked in and sentences were short between mouthfuls. Next came a rice pudding and after that the men had a beer or two.

'Where you been shearing, bro?' asked Jacob.

'Everywhere I can,' Cecil replied. 'Up north, been to NSW, just where I can. I'm paying my way to travel the world.'

'Good, bro,' said another.

'You all shearing the Bowen way?' Cecil asked.

'Yeah, bro, is there any other, eh?' Henry replied.

'Nope, it's the best. Look, sorry, but I'm pretty knackered, so if you don't mind … I need sleep.'

'All good, bro, you might want to go to the dunny before though. It gets really dark here, eh.'

'Thanks, good advice. Ah, is it a seven-thirty start and is there breakfast?' asked Cecil.

'Sure is,' said Larry. 'Six-thirty here, then seven-thirty start.'

'Cheers, see you all tomorrow.'

Cecil could hear laughter as he left and wondered if it was about him. His stomach was churning. He had a searing headache. He ran to his room and locked the door.

'You fucking idiot, you haven't touched a bloody sheep for two fucking years. What are you doing?!'

Chapter 14

By November the grocery shop was becoming even busier. Hector proved to be a treasure and sometimes his wife came to help. Kathleen kept herself occupied by making her sought-after Christmas puddings and cakes they sold at the shop this time of the year. The usual happy get-together would not happen this Christmas. Harold's brother and his family insisted they all spend the day with them, not wanting them to be alone.

After the police left at their last meeting, Harold and Kathleen cried and clung to each other. Was there ever going to be an end to the sorrow they felt every day? The business kept them from dwelling too much; night-time was another matter.

Rebecca was now five and her grandparents continued to be concerned for her. Lillian's swinging moods were becoming more frequent.

Despite all she was dealing with, Kathleen decided to confront Lillian for her granddaughter's sake. Both grandparents loved Rebecca as though she were their own child. They considered Lillian incapable of meeting all her needs. So she chose the day and caught the tram to their house. She gave no warning for the visit.

John answered the door. Both were surprised to see each other.

'You're not at work today?' asked Kathleen.

'Lillian's not well. I'm looking after Rebecca.'

'Grandma, Grandma.' Rebecca appeared from the back of the house and grabbed her grandmother's legs. Kathleen picked her up and held her.

'Where is she, John?' Kathleen asked sternly.

'Um, well—'

'Where is she?' Kathleen repeated.

'She's in bed. She's been there for two days.'

'What?! In bed?' Kathleen's anger was rising. Her anger was a rare thing but this time she was very irritated. 'John, make some tea please. I will see to Lillian.'

John meekly withdrew to the kitchen. Still holding onto Rebecca, Kathleen marched to the bedroom. Clothes were scattered on the floor, the blind was shut and Lillian's uncombed hair was spread haphazardly over the pillows.

'Get up! Get up!'

Lillian turned to see her mother standing over the bed with fury etched on her face.

'What are you doing here? I'm not getting up, I'm sick,' said Lillian indignantly.

With one hand Kathleen pulled back the bed covers. 'Get up now and come to the kitchen.'

Lillian grudgingly obeyed her mother, put on a dressing gown and followed her. They all sat in the kitchen with Rebecca still on Kathleen's knee.

'Alright, what is going on here? You don't seem sick to me.'

'I have a severe headache,' said Lillian.

'Then why didn't you call me?'

'I didn't want to bother you,' replied Lillian.

'Rubbish. That has never worried you before. It's you who rings in the early hours of the morning. You think I don't know?'

'What?' said John, who knew nothing of his wife's mischievous behaviour.

'That's not me.'

'Yes, Lillian, it is, and the whole family is sick of you. What is more important is our little Rebecca here,' she said, giving Rebecca an extra squeeze. 'Things are going to change. Rebecca is going to go to kindergarten.'

Lillian had fought this suggestion for many months. 'She's my daughter and I will decide.'

'No, you won't, Lillian. This little girl is not here to fetch this and that for you. She needs to be cared for properly, loved, able to learn and to play with other children. She is not just your possession to do with as you like. This darling child deserves far better than this.'

'I agree,' said John, who, up to now, had remained silent.

'And what have you done to stop this dreadful situation, John?'

'I work shift work,' he said as justification.

Kathleen ignored him.

'This is what is going to happen. I will walk Rebecca down to kinder today and enroll her. I will give them her parents' details as well as her grandparents'. We will pay any fees due and provide her with the clothing she needs. As it is just down the road, you can walk her there and walk her home. If you don't turn up, I will insist the teacher call us.'

'You can't do that; you can't boss me about and take my daughter.'

'Yes, I can, Lillian. If you don't do this, I will tell the kindergarten, all the family and the church about how you neglect your child. Now, Harold will be here by the time I get back with Rebecca. Go and get dressed.'

Lillian gave her mother a look of insolence as she stomped off to the bedroom.

'She's right, you know, Kathleen; you can't do this.'

'John, why haven't you stepped in and done something about your wife and daughter? You could have told us. We could help.'

'You are still getting over the loss of Pat, Kathleen. I didn't think I could.'

Kathleen didn't reply to his excuses. She knew he didn't care much for any of them.

After washing Rebecca's hands and face, combing her hair and changing her clothes, Kathleen took her hand and walked her down to the kindergarten. The teacher was a gentle woman, who loved and enjoyed preparing the children for primary school through learning and play. The kindergarten had an excellent reputation. Kathleen knew this from talks with some of the customers she had questioned at the grocery shop.

Rebecca was excited and happy to be going to the kindergarten. Holding hands with Kathleen restored her confidence. She never wanted to let go.

It was nearing the end of the kinder day; all the children had left. The teacher was clearing up.

'Hello,' Kathleen said softly, so as not to startle her.

'Oh, hello. Can I help you?'

'Yes, I would like to enroll my granddaughter. My name is Mrs Whitman and this is Rebecca.'

The teacher shook Kathleen's hand then looked down and greeted Rebecca. 'I'm Anne Johnson. You can call me Miss Johnson, Rebecca,' she said with the most generous smile.

Rebecca adored her immediately. Rebecca was invited to play with some of the toys, books and puzzles while the two women talked.

It was too late to enroll her full-time for the remainder of the year, however, Anne Johnson thought it a good idea for her to come for a couple of hours twice a week on a temporary basis so she could be assessed. 'It might be that she is ready for primary school. I wouldn't want to hold her back a year if she is.'

Kathleen wholly agreed. She felt comfortable with Anne Johnson, enough to impart some details of Rebecca's mother. Rather than saying Lillian may be mentally ill (and Kathleen was beginning to think she was), she said Lillian was going through a difficult time due to the death of her sister Patricia.

Anne was quiet for a moment then remembered she had read about this in the papers. 'I am so sorry, Mrs Whitman. This is a dreadful thing to bear.'

'Thank you for your kind words. Rebecca was the first to find her aunt on the rocks,' she whispered.

Anne Johnson gasped and covered her mouth to quieten her dismay. She looked at the little girl, playing over in the corner of the room with all the new books and toys and felt deeply for her. No child should have to deal with that.

All details for Rebecca along with contact phone numbers were dutifully recorded and Rebecca was to come the following Tuesday.

On the way back to the house, Rebecca said, 'Who's going to take me to school, Grandma?'

'It's kindergarten, darling, where you can learn things about going to school next year. Mummy will take you.'

'What if Mummy is sick?

'Then Miss Johnson will tell us and we will take you.'

Rebecca was satisfied with this arrangement and skipped along with her grandmother to the house.

Harold had arrived and was sitting in the kitchen with the recalcitrant Lillian.

'Come here,' she ordered Rebecca. But Rebecca stayed where she was, holding on to her grandmother.

'That way of talking to your daughter will stop now. Do you hear me? I have spoken to the kindergarten and Rebecca will start next Tuesday. If she doesn't arrive, they will contact me. This cannot go on, Lillian. Now, we are taking you to the doctor today. It has been arranged; you need help.'

'I don't need to go to a doctor and I won't,' Lillian replied angrily.

'If you want to keep your daughter, you will.'

Harold took Rebecca to a playground nearby while Kathleen steered Lillian into the family doctor's room, holding her strongly by the arm. He knew the family well. After an hour of consultation, the doctor recommended a psychiatrist and wrote a letter to take with her. He prescribed some tablets for her nerves, as he put it, and she was to start them that day. Contrary to Lillian's errant behavior with her parents and family, she put others in society on a pedestal; doctors were part of that group. In their presence she was respectful and willingly deferred to them. They never observed the real Lillian.

Everyone sat in the kitchen and watched Lillian take her tablets. John had gone to work and Kathleen decided to stay the night and wouldn't leave until she could see an improvement. After a couple of days Lillian was feeling much better and would continue to take her tablets. Kathleen was able to go back to the shop.

Rebecca was dutifully taken to kindergarten, where she spent some of the happiest days of her life.

One day, close to Christmas, Lillian sat Rebecca on her knee and they listened to Bing Crosby on the wireless telling the story of the 'The Small One', a donkey that was destined to be killed at the tanners but was bought by Joseph and carried Mary to Bethlehem. Throughout her life, that rare, precious moment would be remembered.

Chapter 15

Cecil couldn't sleep. It was dark and he was pacing, talking to himself. He went through the process of shearing the Bowen technique, which was done in fifty-five blows. He had done it many times working on his father's sheep farm but he was out of practice and very nervous. He held an imaginary comb in his hand and stepped through it, holding an imaginary sheep between his legs.

Left hand takes sheep's leg, first blow down round the inside flank, next round under the leg, then the other side of the flank, down the belly stretching the skin, complete the belly, down the top of the leg, covering the teats, inside the crotch to the centre, across the crotch to the other leg, complete the crotch, then top of leg, into the flank, straight down the firm part of leg, straight down leg, under the tail, up the back, top of the head, eye clips over each eye, back of ear, step through to brisket, down the shoulder, straight up under throat, side of other cheek, under ear, first shoulder, sock of stretched leg, few short blows up the back then long blows, roll sheep around, other cheek, down to brisket, last side down to the leg.

If anyone had witnessed this performance, they would have thought he was practising a religious ritual. In a way, he was.

Next morning, Cecil, dressed in shearer's clothes and, wearing his cap, arrived in the kitchen at six-thirty. The others were already there eating breakfasts of porridge and toast. There was a pot of tea on the wood stove.

'Hi, bro,' they said, through mouths full of food. 'How'd you sleep?'

'All good,' he said.

'Come and have something to eat,' said Larry.

Cecil sat down and put some toast on his plate. He would try to eat but his stomach was still in revolt.

'I suppose you're familiar with the hours?' asked Larry.

'Seven-thirty to nine-thirty, ten to twelve, one to three and three-thirty to five-thirty. Is that right?'

'Correct, mate,' Larry confirmed.

There was lots of chatter and camaraderie amongst the men. It was warm in here and somewhere in the room an old fridge rattled, the fire crackled, outside sheep were bleating, dogs were barking and Cecil's heart was once again racing. Practising the previous night had given him a modicum of confidence but not enough to quell his anxiety. Just before they started, the shearers did a few stretching exercises outside. Cecil copied them, as if he had always done it.

Once inside the shed at seven-thirty am the shearing began with their hand pieces. Cecil dragged his first sheep from the catching pen to the raised board. He positioned the sheep upright between his legs and began. His hand was shaking but no one noticed. He made a couple of small errors and he was slower than the others but the process came back to him. Years of shearing with his father had paid off. His first shorn sheep was ejected through the porthole and down the chute. A roustabout came out of nowhere, picked up the fleece and took it to the wool table for skirting. The other shearers were already onto their third sheep. Larry, the ringer, was ahead of them all. Cecil didn't have time to worry. He dragged in the next sheep. By the end of the first quarter, he was starting to catch up with the others.

At nine-thirty, during the smoko, he was feeling pretty good.

'You're doing good, bro. Sweet as,' said one of the shearers.

'Cheers, bro,' said Cecil.

These men were lean and very fit. If you lined them all up, Cecil looked like the runt of the litter, plus, he always wore his silly cap over his long hair. He hadn't shaved for months. Initially the men were suspicious of him but today he proved his worth.

The shearing shed was a smelly hot place with constant noise. The men talked all the time – some of it was bad language. Things like, 'Fuck, bro, what's wrong with you today?' or, 'You need a root mate, that'll fix you up, eh'. And there was always talk about looking forward to the next piss-up and who chundered last time. Even so, these were good men working at a hard job to support families. The kidding around was a release and accepted as such.

Lunch was soup and bread in the kitchen. They were given a tin that contained a fruitcake for the afternoon break, with strict orders from the cook to bring the tin back.

By the end of the day Cecil had shorn one hundred and twenty sheep. Although he didn't show it, his body was wracked with pain; every single muscle burned, especially his back and arms.

This time, tea was roast lamb with potatoes. Cecil was in agony but his hunger was stronger. He couldn't stay for pudding.

Back in his room he took two strong tablets and lay down. He didn't bother to wash or undress; he went to sleep almost straight away.

The same routine went on for two weeks. Cecil averaged two hundred sheep a day. Larry around two hundred and fifty. He was admired but no one told him that.

The shearing was finished and all the sheep were now out in the paddocks. That night, a lot of drinking took place. Cecil kept his wits about him. He would not slip up.

On the fifteenth day, cheques were handed out, all made out to cash. Cecil had earned eighty-four pounds and twelve shillings. He had enjoyed his time at the station and most times he was able to erase what he did. The owner of the sheep station, Tom Barker, came to shake hands and farewell the shearers. He peered at Cecil a fraction longer than the others. 'Have we met?' he asked.

'No, I would remember if we had,' replied Cecil, hoping he sounded convincing.

They all boarded the TSS Earnslaw that morning. In Queenstown they said their goodbyes. Cecil was the only one catching the bus back to Dunedin, for which he was grateful.

The next day, the newspapers that arrived at the sheep station contained an article about a man wanted for questioning in Hobart, Tasmania. It was on the front page along with a photo of Cecil. The photo bore no resemblance at all to the long-haired, bearded man who left the day before.

He arrived back at the house at Port Chalmers late in the afternoon. After dropping off his bags, checking the house and the van he walked to the post office and cashed his cheque. A telegram was waiting for him from Edward Martin saying he may be in Antarctica for another three to four months, longer than intended. Cecil sent one back.

All good here. Stop. Not in a hurry to go. Stop. Enjoying Port Chalmers. Stop. Good luck with it all. Stop. Norman.

He purchased a newspaper, food, toiletries and washing powder. He needed to wash his clothes and he desperately needed a bath. First though, he started up the van, to make sure the battery hadn't gone flat. It turned over and he gave a sigh of relief. Then he turned and looked at the view. The house faced the south-western Pacific Ocean. He appreciated it more than the first time. The wind was blowing; he could just see the waves and a couple of ships. A few tears ran down his cheeks, he wasn't sure why. Maybe he was tired, relieved, remorseful or feeling self-pity.

He went inside, ran a bath and turned on the radio. He unpacked and shoved dirty clothes into the washing machine for later. He pulled clean pyjamas from a drawer, checked the water temperature of the bath and climbed in. Holding his breath, he totally immersed himself, only coming back up when his breath ran out. After scrubbing his whole body, he finally got out and dried himself. He found himself humming to a song that was playing. What was that song? It evoked something. *Oh Christ, 'Harbour Lights'*. He'd danced with Pat to this music.

Keeping busy was his way to forget. Forget Pat, forget about his bleak childhood, forget questioning himself. He wanted peace of mind. He washed his clothes, cleaned up the house and cooked a meal. Tomorrow he would take a drive in the van, have another look around.

After tea he looked at the paper. There it was, a photo of Cecil Newton, wanted for questioning in Tasmania. Panic enveloped him again. After a moment he forced himself to take another look. The man gazing back was nothing like the Cecil of today. He had more hair now. He'd just tidied it all but it was still long enough to hide his real identity. He had lost weight; his cheeks were hollower and his skin was darker due to more hours outside and he had aged. He was certain Cecil Newton would no longer be recognised. Nonetheless, after seeing the article, he decided to bunker down in Port Chalmers well into the New Year.

There was something else. He couldn't contact his father, ever again. Anyway, his father wouldn't care. All through his childhood he'd tried, but deep down he knew his father didn't like him.

Chapter 16

Christmas day came and went. In light of everything that happened it wasn't the same but having family around meant everything to Harold and Kathleen. Lillian and John seemed more relaxed and talkative and Rebecca played with the other children.

It was now January 1953 with no more news of Cecil Newton. Everyone began to believe there never would be. It was anathema for them to think it, but in this case, they hoped he was dead.

The kindergarten teacher had written a glowing report about Rebecca. She had observed her closely and found she enjoyed learning, learnt quickly, could read well, knew her numbers and had positive interactions with other children or she could happily amuse herself. She had mental and emotional strength and wisdom beyond her years. She had drawn pictures of her family and named the largest figured positioned at the front of the group as her aunty Pat. Anne Johnson found her to be a very sweet, obliging child and wished her well. The report was sent to the headmistress along with all contacts for the child. Carbon copies were sent to her parents and grandparents.

Rebecca was enrolled at the local primary school and was to start Tuesday third of February in the kindergarten program, three hours a day, three days a week. The kindergarten teacher, who had trained at the Teachers College in Victoria, was said to have excellent credentials, something else Kathleen had been told by some of the customers at the shop.

Members of the family would do transport duties as there was no direct buses or trams from Augusta Road to the school. During the warmer days Lillian and Rebecca would very occasionally walk to Elizabeth Street, catch a tram to Burnett Street and walk the rest of the way to school. Sometimes her father would drive her but this was rare. The main responsibility fell to her grandfather and her second cousin, Hector, neither of who minded at all. They would always take her back to the shop after kindergarten, where she would sit at the table out the back, have a cake, sandwich or a piece of fruit and tell her family about her day.

'Do you still like kindergarten?' asked Kathleen constantly.

'Yes, Grandma, I like it.'

'What did you do today?'

'I played with blocks and I was singing and I did a drawing.' She pulled it out of her bag and unfolded it to show. 'That's you, Grandma, and that's Grandpa and that's the shop.'

Kathleen hugged her and told her how clever she was. When the time came to go home, she never revealed how sad she was to be leaving them.

After a year of kindergarten, Rebecca was ready for grade one. Her teacher gave a glowing report of a child who was well-mannered, cooperative and popular with her peers. She noted her favourite subject was reading and that she had excellent comprehension and good drawing skills for her age. The teacher also noted Rebecca sometimes had quiet moments and this could be the result of reliving a tragedy she witnessed last year. It was recommended this habit of retreating be monitored closely. She finished the report by wishing Rebecca all the very best for her future at Hill Street Primary School.

Harold and Kathleen bought everything Rebecca needed for her first day in grade one. She had her uniform and the books and pencils she needed. Kathleen helped her cover a couple of her small books in brown paper.

Lillian had regressed and was back in bed some days. It was becoming obvious she had some sort of personality disorder. John took her to the doctor again and she was prescribed different tablets. None of these drugs made any real difference to her demeanour for long. She had another letter to take to a psychiatrist but she refused to go. John was becoming frustrated with her and worked longer hours, delaying his time to go home.

She had her good days, then she would take Rebecca to school and be invited by the teacher to look over some of the things her daughter had done in class. Her reaction was never as enthusiastic as her daughter would have wished. Other mothers were simply gushing over their children's efforts. Her grandparents were very interested though and praised Rebecca daily.

There was a highlight in that year. Rebecca's school arranged for pupils to be taken to the city to wave flags for Queen Elizabeth II who was visiting. It was hard to see her at times but it was an exciting day and Rebecca couldn't stop talking about it when she came home. She described the Queen's clothes and pretty face, the car she was in, the lines of the children all waving their flags and how happy she was to be in the city with its trees and some tall buildings. She described how she could have stayed there forever. Lillian listened but made no comment nor shared her daughter's enthusiasm. She simply got up from the table and started to prepare a meal.

Months were passing quickly and Rebecca enjoyed every minute. She had friends but her special and most devoted was a boy called Timothy (he preferred to be called Tim) and they gravitated to each other from the start. Tim's father was an accountant and his mother managed a women's dress shop. There was no doubt of the love they had for their only son.

It was nearing the end of the year. Rebecca was now six and Tim a month older. A decision was made by both sets of parents, Harold and Kathleen, that the two children could walk together after school to the shop, which was located near the corner of Letitia Street. It included traffic lights and it was a short, safe distance from the school. This was a highlight of their day and they talked on this walk about the teacher, the lesson of the day, games they played like marbles, skipping, paddy cake paddy cake, along with opinions of their peers in a language only six-year-olds could understand.

Tim was always welcome to stay a while at the shop where both children would continue their conversation along with a piece of cake or sandwich.

'I think she's silly,' said Rebecca about one of the girls in their class. 'She giggles all the time and doesn't do her drawings properly. She smells too.'

'Do you like your grandma and grandpa?' Tim inquired, ignoring her comments.

'Yes, I do, I love them lots,' she replied between bites of her sandwich and the swinging of her legs.

'Do you love your mummy and daddy?' he asked innocently.

She thought for a moment, contemplating her answer. 'Not much,' she said.

'I love my mummy and daddy lots too,' he said, not really hearing her comment.

Neither could proffer reasons about the comments they just made; they were too young for in-depth explanations. All they knew was how they felt.

After a time, Tim was walked back by Harold to his parent's house in Smith Street, which was also close to the grocery shop. This child was always warmly welcomed home by his father, who in turn thanked Harold. The difference between the welcome in this house to that of Lillian and John was obvious.

At the end of the school year, Harold, Kathleen, Lillian and John were invited to afternoon tea by Tim's mother Mabel to celebrate their children's success. Rebecca and Tim had done well in the first year. It was a well-meaning attempt to meet Rebecca's parents. John excused himself due to work and Lillian said she was unwell.

John was not one to use the telephone often. But this time he had made an exception. He used his work commitments as an excuse and said Lillian was sick. Neither was true. Dealing with Lillian sapped his energy, dragged him down. He was not in the mood to pretend all was well.

Again, it was left to the grandparents to take the place of her absent parents. Mabel and her husband Robert knew this wonderful couple from the grocery shop and despite, or because of, Rebecca's parents' absence the day went well. There was enjoyable discussion and contentment. Rebecca hadn't witnessed her grandparents' delighted smiles for a long time. She was happy to see it and to be with her best friend, Tim.

Chapter 17

Celebrations and the observance of the New Year of 1953 passed by Cecil in a whimper. He visited the local pub on a couple of occasions but not during the celebrations. He was always looking over his shoulder expecting the dreaded tap any moment. Keeping low had proved to be the best strategy.

He keenly read newspapers, finding it a stimulating pastime. His desire for further education had been blocked by his hardheaded father who thought academia was for elitists. Sheep farming was practical. His plans for his son's future on the sheep station were set and indefatigable. Cecil strived to please his father but remained undeterred in his thirst for knowledge and read hungrily in his spare time.

He wrote an opinion piece on the New Zealand political climate at the time, signing it anonymously while providing his current address to the editor. It was an excellent piece of writing and his bipartisanship and logical analysis were evident. A letter was sent back to Cecil saying his piece would be published in the paper the following week and, if he were to write more, they would be happy to pay.

Cecil did continue to write on many subjects, including sport, shipping, housing, education and the progressive inclusion of women in the police force and juries. He received payments for these articles, by cheque made out to cash as requested. For the first time in many months, he felt he was doing something worthwhile and enjoyed finally using this skill that had been sacrificed to appease his father.

Ironically, he saw his father's death notice one day during his readings. He had died in hospital from a brain hemorrhage. The death notice asked for any relative to contact the funeral parlour so they could go ahead with burial arrangements. Cecil was the only relative, but for obvious reasons he couldn't reveal it. He did, however, send off a money order to cover some of the costs and suggested his father be buried beside his wife, Mrs Jane Newton, who had died June 1943. He couldn't give his name or address. All he could do was hope this would be done. It was a sad moment for Cecil; despite their taciturn relationship, there was regret and questioning. Could it have been different? After a couple of days of silent mourning he resumed the business of writing.

It was now the end of February; time was moving on and Cecil still had no idea of what to do next. Edward would be back soon and then what? He continued to read the newspapers almost halfheartedly while considering his future. Then he noticed it, a small item received from America. It started *Rec. 8.00pm* then recounted the story about a man who had changed his gender to a woman. She had become famous in the United States. He read and re-read the article several times. Hair stood up on the back of his neck; his head felt on fire. Suddenly, he stood up, knocked over his chair and paced around the room for a long time. This was a revelation. He was always aware of a feminine gentleness within him but fear of rejection and his own self-denial would squash it. Deep down, he knew the reason why he had never been able to consummate any of his relationships with women, even Pat. And it was why his father never felt close to his son. Cecil didn't sleep that night. The article he just read gave him the impetus to find if he could be what he secretly always wanted – to be female.

The next day he packed up all his belongings and locked the van. He put any monies owed in the secret place he and Edward had organised. He wrote a long letter thanking Edward for everything, locked up the house, put the keys in the other safe place and walked to the post office to cash his latest postal order. He caught a train to Dunedin then changed to a goods train going to Christchurch. It seemed to take forever but he finally arrived mid-afternoon. He arranged passage on a flight to Sydney for the next day then booked a room for the night in a hotel. His sleep was sporadic again but this time it was due to excitement and hope.

In the morning he caught a taxi to the airport and boarded the plane. As it took off, he looked out over the islands of New Zealand and hoped he would never return as Cecil.

After a rather longer than expected flight, Cecil arrived at Sydney Airport and caught a bus into the city. He had visited Sydney before on his way to Tasmania, but only briefly. He needed to look around, get his bearings. Booking into a hotel was first on his list.

He finished unpacking and sat on the bed with a map and newspaper with the intention of finding a place to rent. He found something of interest in Cooper Street, Surrey Hills.

No one was using the bathroom located at the end of the long hall in the hotel, so he took the opportunity to wash and trim his beard, moustache and hair. It was a basic bathroom with a yellow basin and a bath. Some of the enamel had flaked off and the mirror was showing its age with odd patches of rust. Steam had affected parts of the walls and mould was appearing in places near the ceiling. Cecil didn't care; he had the room all to himself. The face in the mirror looked back at him. There were lines appearing around the mouth and pain in his eyes. Scrubbing again didn't improve it. With a deep sigh he went back to his room and changed into his suit, which didn't fit him well anymore. He hadn't been able to gain his weight back. He donned his cap, feeling more secure with it in place and went to the estate agent.

Yes, the flat in Cooper Street was still vacant and yes, he could have a look at it. It was an old Victorian terrace and obviously hadn't been lived in for some time but with a cleanup Cecil could see its potential. It included a few pieces of furniture, a working stove and the rent was pretty reasonable. A lease was signed, with the bond and four months rent in advance paid in cash. He could move in as soon as he liked. No other questions were asked of him.

Back at the hotel he started a list of things he needed. At this stage it would only be the minimum; he had to reduce his spending until he found an avenue of income. After that he went downstairs for something to eat then back to his room for rest. It was quiet and his thoughts turned to how long he had been on the run, places he'd been and if he would ever be able to live without fear. He was hopeful, he could envisage a chance to completely change and be the person he forbade himself to be since he could remember. His thoughts inevitably returned to Pat.

The next few days were spent finding pieces of basic furniture, a small fridge, a few tools and, importantly, a typewriter and wireless. Some items were already marked down due to slight damage and yet he still bargained. He arranged the connection of gas and electricity. Furniture was placed, he cleaned up, fixed treads on the rickety stairs, catches on windows and locks on doors. The final thing was to secure a hiding place for his cash; he chose a floorboard under the stairs.

He needed a phone. He filled out the form and one was installed within a couple of weeks. It began to irritate him that he still had to use a false name; it meant he couldn't use any of the formal identification he had hidden along with his cash, his birth certificate and driver's licence.

He found a doctor in Bourke Street a short distance from his flat. He walked to the doctor's rooms and made an appointment for the next day at a quarter to eleven. To say he was edgy was nowhere near it; he was so fearful he nearly turned back. He stood still for a moment, took stock of himself and arrived ten minutes early. The receptionist showed him in.

Doctor Paterson was sitting in a most luxurious, high-backed leather chair at a beautifully polished table with a green, leather insert in the centre. Everything in the room was clean and orderly. They greeted each other and Cecil used his real name, secure in the knowledge of confidentiality in this room.

'What's wrong, Mr Newton? Where do you feel unwell?' said the slow-speaking doctor who emphasised *unwell* along with a tone of superiority. This had the effect of unsettling Cecil.

'Well, I …'

'Take your time. Now, do you think you have a fever or are you in pain?' The doctor was now looking down at his writing pad, pen paused, waiting.

'No, none of those. I want to ask about something else.'

'Yes, go ahead,' he said, still staring at his pad.

'I want to become a woman.' It was the first time he had spoken of it to anyone.

Dr Paterson finally put down his pen and lifted his head.

Looking squarely at Cecil, he said, 'Are you sure?'

'All my life.' Cecil had to take control of tears that sprang up in the corner of his tired eyes.

'I see. Well, I can't help you. I'm Catholic; it's against everything I believe. However, I pass no judgement on you, of course.' His tone was becoming kinder now. 'I'm going to give you a letter to take to a colleague I know who is sympathetic to your wishes.'

'Thank you, Doctor,' Cecil said, in a tone that was bordering on obsequiousness.

There was complete silence. The doctor's scrawls seemed amplified in the quiet room. He put the letter in an envelope, addressed it and handed it to Cecil. It was for a specialist in Macquarie Street.

'I have to tell you: you are starting on a very audacious medical expedition, Cecil. There will be months of psychiatric assessment. If, after that, you qualify, there will be medication that you may have to take for the remainder of your life. And, of course, there is the public perception. Many may reject you from their circle.'

'I understand,' said Cecil, fighting his emotions.

'There's no fee for today,' he said, shaking Cecil's hand. 'I wish you the best of luck.'

'Thank you, Doctor, thank you.'

Cecil ran all the way back to his flat. He sat on the couch and wept. He was about to embark on the most important moment of his life. It would change him, forever. He wrestled with it for hours, waking up, walking around the floor and thinking, thinking. Would it work? Was it safe? How would he look and behave? After a few days he decided he wanted this more than anything, always had. He made an appointment with the doctor in Macquarie Street and was travelling on a bus for his first consultation. He was calmer about his decision but concern still hung around him like a thick, heavy coat. The clinic's reception area was rather lavish and he started wondering how much this was going to cost.

Dr Miller, wearing a colourful bow tie and black suit, came out in person and invited him in. His room was tastefully filled with works of art, small artefacts on modern shelving and light-coloured leather chairs.

'Have a seat. Cecil, is it?'

'Yes, that's right,' said Cecil, feeling vulnerable.

'You have a letter for me, I believe?'

'Oh, sorry, yes.' He searched his pockets. Where the hell had he put it? Finally it was produced.

The doctor read it and nodded his head, saying, 'Hmm' now and then, indicating complete agreement with the content.

'Right, well I believe you have felt like this all your life.'

'Yes.'

'And you're sure you want to go ahead?'

'Without a doubt.'

'Well, the first thing to be done is you have to see a psychiatrist.'

'I don't understand. Why?' said Cecil, perplexed.

'We need to be absolutely sure this is what you want, that there are no other underlying issues that would cause you to regret your decision further down the track, so to speak.'

'I see. I don't know if I can afford all this.'

'We can consider special circumstances,' said Dr Miller.

'I'm not asking for free consultations but I can't pay a lot either. I do have experience in journalism which is my ultimate goal, but I'm new here and need to find other work in between time.'

'Have a talk to the psychiatrist about it. I'm sure you'll find him a reasonable man.'

'Alright, thank you. What's the next step?'

'I'll write a letter to him. I envisage you will only need a month with him. You're an adult; you seem to genuinely know how you feel and what you want to do about it. I can't see he will need any more time than that.' Dr Miller was smiling in an effort to make his patient less tense. 'He's just up the road from here. You live in Cooper Street, Surrey Hills?'

'Yes, just a small old Victorian cottage, but it suits me.'

'You don't have far to travel, good, good. I'll just write this note for you and I suggest you take it straight to his clinic now and make an appointment. The sooner we start this the better for you, I suspect.'

'Yes,' said Cecil with a nervous smile. He was very appreciative of his understanding.

'I would like to advise you about one thing. It is preferable that you don't talk to anyone about this treatment. It's in its infancy. Don't be alarmed, it is safe, but many in the profession are not admirers of it, shall we say. It goes against some of their principles. And some people in the public domain don't agree with it either.'

'I have no intention of telling a soul,' said Cecil, and he meant it.

'Good,' replied his doctor.

Dr Miller was correct; the psychiatrist was only six doors away. The appointment was made for the following Monday at one pm.

Sitting in the bus on his way back home, Cecil was feeling a mix of emotions. Exaltation, dread, happiness, dread again. Ultimately though, he was jubilant. His deepest desire was going to be fulfilled, after all this time.

Chapter 18

Time rolled on for Rebecca and her family. Lillian had her ups and downs. She had bad days where she stayed in bed. The doctor would prescribe something else and she would be her better self again, but it didn't last for long. John was hardly around; he didn't want to be. Harold and Kathleen worked relentlessly at their shop; it kept sorrow at bay.

Rebecca's love of school hadn't faded: she always attained good marks and cherished the red ticks, stars, stamps and the positive comments written on the pages. She liked most of her teachers, except one in grade four, Miss Reid. This teacher was brusque and a strict disciplinarian. She could smack a hand with her ruler on her way to the front of the class and think nothing of it, leaving the receiver of her punishment bewildered.

Rebecca had a strong sense of right and wrong and one day, she questioned her.

'Why did you do that?' she exclaimed. 'I haven't done anything wrong.'

'You were not concentrating, child.'

'Yes, I was.'

'Don't contradict or speak to me like that again.' She came up to Rebecca with her ruler raised, ready to strike.

'You can't smack us for nothing. You just can't do that.'

This enraged Miss Reid so much she missed her target and ended up hitting Rebecca right across her face. It was the end of the school day and all were dismissed.

'What happened, Bec?' asked Tim as they walked home.

She told him and he held her hand. 'We will have a cake at the shop soon,' Tim said. He didn't know how else to console her.

The red welt was now a red line imprinted on her face. All at the shop were horrified. She was held and kissed by her caring grandparents. 'Thank you for helping her, Tim,' said Harold, giving him a gentle pat on his back.

The next day Harold, Kathleen and Lillian took Rebecca straight to the headmistress' office.

She was shocked and summoned Miss Reid.

'What is the meaning of this?' she asked, showing the side of Rebecca's face.

'She was becoming undisciplined,' said Miss Reid with her raised chin, assured she was justified in dealing out her punishments.

'Collect your things and leave the school grounds immediately. I have had one too many complaints about you – you're dismissed.'

'You can't do that.'

'Yes, I can. If you don't like it, go and complain to the board. I suspect you won't though.'

Miss Reid was never seen again. On that day, the headmistress took the class and it was the best the grade four's ever had.

Onlookers would say Rebecca wasn't always perfect. There was taunting in the playground from others at times, then she would fight. She had a quick temper and an obstinacy that didn't always serve her well. But this part of her character rarely surfaced.

She and Tim were still close friends and never argued. They didn't see a lot of each other when in school. Pupil numbers grew, so some classes were split into two groups. The children chose their own groups in the playground. It was an unspoken rule: the boys played with the boys and the girls with the girls. But walking home together after school never stopped.

There came a time when Rebecca and Tim didn't need family to take them to and from school or walk Tim home. They were both eleven and in grade six; it was nearing the end of the school year. Both were allowed a certain amount of freedom providing they came back at agreed times and family always knew where they were.

One day after school both were at Tim's house. His mother Mabel was home. She brought in a plate of sliced cake and fruit to the table where the children were talking about the end of year exams and starting at Hobart High School in Letitia Street the following year. It was a short walk away from the shop and Tim's place.

They were a little sad at leaving their primary school, it was a known quantity and they both liked it there. Excitement and anticipation were also a part of their talk. Their teacher had talked to them about some of the subjects they may be studying next year. English, Australian history, geography and cookery were some mentioned. There was also maths and science. They couldn't remember all she spoke about but it was enough to send their imaginative minds into a heightened state.

'I like the maths and science best,' said Tim.

'I like English and history,' said Rebecca. 'I want to teach it one day.'

'I didn't know that.' Tim was surprised.

'I've just decided,' she said.

'I'm not sure what I'm going to do. I don't want to be an accountant. My uncle is an engineer, I might do that,' said Tim.

'What does he do?'

'Not sure. He talks to Dad sometimes about telescopes, I've heard him. I'll ask Dad.'

Voices were heard in the kitchen, then silence. Hector and Mabel walked into the room.

'Hello, Hector. I can walk back to the shop, you don't have to do it.'

His eyes looked watery.

Rebecca smiled at her second cousin. 'What's wrong with your eyes?'

Hector moved closer and bent down to her. 'Bec, your grandpa just died.' Tears were on his face now and he looked crestfallen.

Rebecca stood up suddenly. 'But I saw him this morning, he was looking better.' She was shocked, distraught and disbelieving. Why didn't she realise how sick he was? Why didn't someone tell her? She loved him so much.

Tim and his mother sat down at the table; they were speechless.

Hector put his arms around her. She started to cry and couldn't stop. He held onto her and put her into the car and drove the short drive to her grandparents' house.

Rebecca entered the house and ran to her grandmother. They held each other and cried.

Harold had been in an out of hospital in the last two months with pain in his stomach. The hospital decided to remove his appendix and he seemed to be getting better. It turned out it was worse than that. Kathleen didn't tell anyone but he had cancer. The doctor's prognosis was that he didn't have long. She nursed him along with some help from Lillian and other women in the extended family. Sometime that morning he'd closed his eyes and didn't wake. It was 1959; he was only fifty-seven.

The funeral service was held at St James' Anglican Church, New Town. Harold was well known. As well as his administrative duties at the church there were many people from the Taroona community and the grocery shop that remembered him. They came to offer their condolences and speak at the service. Hector and his wife Lilly stood at the entrance to thank people and give them a program for the service. It was standing room inside the church and overflowing. Some people had to listen from outside.

Kathleen, Lillian, John and Rebecca were already seated in the front pew. Rebecca had asked if Tim could sit beside her and Tim's parents sat directly behind. There was also an open coffin and before the service many people came up to say goodbye to Harold. Some kissed his forehead, some patted his cold hand, men doffed their hats and women lovingly touched his coffin.

The minister started the service with a hymn, 'Nearer My God to Thee' by Sarah Flower Adams. Next, everyone joined in saying the twenty-third psalm. The minister spoke benevolently of Harold, listing his virtues, his wonderful works, his joyful presence, his generosity and even his whistling out of tune. All laughed at this as they remembered.

He said, 'A truly kind man has now left this world and gone to God and we shall all miss him greatly.'

Others were invited to speak and a few men did. Caring words were spoken about Harold and all at that service were blowing their noses and wiping their eyes.

The service finished with the hymn, 'Praise the Lord the King of Heaven' by Henry Francis Lyte. Rebecca remembered her grandfather liked all hymns but the two sang today were his favourites. Although she hadn't said it, Rebecca didn't really trust in God anymore but she went to the coffin and put in a photo of her and her grandfather together with some flowers like the ones he used to grow in Taroona, just in case God did exist. She took a long look at his kind face and quietly said goodbye.

The women stayed behind while male relatives went with the coffin to the cemetery. Afternoon tea was held in the hall at the back of the church and, as always, there were sandwiches, cakes of all kinds and cups of tea. Food was put aside for the men on their return.

The time came to go home. Hector and his family took the women back to the house. John drove his car back to Augusta Road; he didn't consider he could help any further and had to start work very early the next morning.

There was a week of mourning, visitors coming and going and those in the house bursting into tears often, day and night. Kathleen and Lillian insisted Rebecca go back to school. She had exams coming up soon and Grandpa wouldn't want her to fail because of him. She didn't want to but in the end she found it better to be distracted. Tim stayed around her at school as much as he could and they resumed walking home together. He was always dependable, her unerring support.

The teacher was more than willing to take the death of her grandfather into consideration when marking her exam, but it wasn't necessary. Rebecca was determined not to let her much-loved grandfather down. She passed top of her class. Tim, who was in the other additional grade six class, came an equal first with another pupil.

Kathleen was a strong woman. After two weeks she decided to go back to work at the shop. It was her saviour when Patricia died and it would be again. Lillian came too, to do the bookwork. Bookkeeping was one thing she could do well and, besides, she could be with her mother, as she always wanted.

Kathleen was not one to hate, but now more than ever, she hated Cecil. In her mind Harold died far too early because of what had been done to their daughter. She absolutely believed it. She hoped that if Cecil were alive somewhere, he was suffering.

Chapter 19

On Monday at one pm Cecil was sitting in the rooms of Dr Peter Wilson, psychiatrist, waiting. He had arrived early because he didn't want to pace around his flat any longer.

'Just get on the bus and get on with it,' he lectured to himself.

There were some information pamphlets and a couple of magazines in the waiting room. He picked them up one by one and tried to read. Instead he nervously flipped through the pages, his eyes not clearly seeing the print.

Dr Wilson finally appeared. He was a tall man in his fifties, dark brown hair, blue eyes, smooth complexion and wearing a well-fitted, tailored, grey suit.

'Sorry to keep you waiting,' he said, with a slight accent that sounded Scandinavian.

Cecil stood up. 'That's alright. Dr Wilson, is it?'

'Yes, yes. Apologies, I am Dr Wilson and you are Mr Newton, correct? Do come in.'

He pointed Cecil towards another room. This room was very welcoming. It had a leather couch, a desk with a leather chair and another chair facing the couch. There were comfortable cushions resting on some of the furniture and Persian rugs covered most of the polished floorboards.

This time Cecil had his letter ready from Dr Miller. 'This is for you,' he said, handing over the envelope.

'Thank you.' He read the letter as if he were meditating. 'Right, I see,' he said knowingly. 'As Dr Miller informed you, these sessions establish that your decision to change gender is resolute.'

'Yes, I understand. Before we start, I want to discuss your fee. I'm not sure if Dr Miller mentioned that in the letter.'

'Yes, he did, and considering your circumstances I can lower my fee to five pounds per session. I envisage one visit a week for a month. It may take longer, of course, but at this stage I think that will suffice.'

'Right, thank you, Doctor,' said Cecil.

'Let's begin then.'

The next few weeks were tough for Cecil. Many of the probing questions asked made him feel self-conscious and uneasy. His character and emotions were exposed and explored. It was like stripping bark from a tree to find yet another, then another. Questions asked were what was the relationship with his parents, relationships with women, relationships with men? Did he masturbate? What sexual fantasies did he have and how did he see himself as a woman in the future? Did he feel anger? Did he feel adrift? At times he felt so wrung out after these sessions, on arriving home he just lay down for hours. As defenseless as he felt, he was never tempted to speak about his time in Tasmania.

During all this he had found work at a warehouse. He was to fill in while someone was sick. He asked to be paid in cash and the company was happy to do it, providing he didn't go to the union. The money helped. Although he was still thin, he looked much healthier in the face now. He had trimmed more off his beard and hair and continued to wear his cap.

Everyone at the warehouse was friendly and talkative, but if too much was asked about Cecil's life he would shut them down. He was so polite and good at it by now they didn't notice his hesitancy in revealing himself.

At the final session Dr Wilson declared Cecil had been suffering from gender dysphoria for years and was, indeed, well-suited and ready for change. He wrote to Dr Miller, smiled, vigorously shook hands with Cecil and wished him the best for his future. Cecil felt elated, as if he had passed an exam in school and received a high distinction mark.

The following week Cecil was back with Dr Miller discussing his treatment. He was to start estrogen hormone therapy in tablet form and would need to see the doctor weekly for a while. He explained what to expect in the coming months: some discomfort around the nipple area, re-distribution of fat to his hips, less muscle definition in his arms and legs, body hair gradually becoming much finer, however, some would always remain. He would also go through emotional changes not unlike puberty and therefore was to expect mood swings, changes in odour, less sweating and the shrinking of his testicles. As well as these changes he would regularly need to have liver and diabetes checks and was advised to exercise as much as possible.

Cecil continued to work at the warehouse for the next three weeks. He noticed some slight changes during this period and decided to stop working there before those changes became obvious. He stayed home most of the time but would venture out to pay bills at the post office, buy food, necessities and visit the doctor. Soon, he realised that no one took any notice of him and he began to feel more self-assured, even visiting the city centre more often and finding a bar to have a beer. He dyed his hair a sort of reddish colour and completely shaved off his beard and moustache. His cap still remained on his head when he went out though; it was his last piece of security. He had, at times, suffered through the hormone therapy. Often, he was an emotional wreck and parts of his body were sore to touch.

At one of his appointments with the doctor, he asked if he would witness a form for a request of a change of name certificate. He was happy to do so. Cecil wanted to be called Mary Taylor. The request was sent to the Land Titles Office and returned to Cecil within three weeks. He was so thrilled about it he rang his doctor straight away to tell him.

Shortly after, he asked Dr Miller if he would come with him for support to open a bank account. The doctor had a friend who was a bank manager so, one day, he and the now Mary Taylor met with him. Along with viewing the change of name document and signing a Statutory Declaration nothing else was required. She had brought along fifty pounds to deposit into her new account. It was a start.

There was other business that had to be done regarding her new name. She went to the offices of the utilities companies and produced her name change document. There were some raised eyebrows but the billing name was eventually changed. The estate agent didn't even blink. Here was an excellent tenant, that's all that mattered to him.

Mary now started to write opinion pieces to the leading newspaper of the time. Politics was her main interest and she wrote her views of the incumbent labour party and liberal party politicians. She posted them along with her name and address. The response from the editor was very positive so she continued to write once a week. The editor decided the paper was happy to pay her a few pounds for her articles. It was asked if she was an independent journalist and her bank details. She lied about the first and gave details of the other.

As time went on, the change from Cecil to Mary Taylor was physically astounding. Small breasts had developed, hips were more distinct, facial and body hair very fine as to be almost invisible and any that were was shaved off. More importantly, she felt what she had always wanted to be – a woman.

It was now early May 1953. Mary needed feminine clothes. First, she visited a thrift shop. Here she could search amongst the women's clothing section without being bothered by inquisitive shop assistants. She chose beige pants. Mary was still thin and it looked like they could fit. The lower part of the pants was wide – they looked comfortable. She also found a blue blouse and a white blouse with a soft fluted collar. To finish the ensemble, she chose a dark navy jacket that had gold buttons on the front and on the sleeves. She found some shoes with a small heel. There was a cabinet in the shop that displayed some costume jewellery. A necklace caught her eye along with a matching bracelet. Then, as she was about to go to the counter, she spied a beret. This all cost a fraction of what it would be if new. She then went to one of the department stores and purchased some make-up.

Her excitement was barely contained while sitting on the bus on the way home. On arrival, she closed and locked the door and went straight to the bedroom where there was a stand-alone mirror in the corner. Mary put on her clothes in haste, impatient to see the result of her purchases. The final touch was the jewellery. She gently put the necklace around her neck and the bracelet on her wrist, then slowly turned around to the mirror. At that moment, she imagined a magic wand had been waved over her. She was a completely different person. A belt was needed for the pants, the jacket fitted well, as did the two blouses. She needed something under the rather transparent material but that could be done and maybe some stockings wouldn't go astray.

Over the next few days Mary practised applying makeup. She had closely studied women's faces on the bus and in the street. On the first few tries she looked like a clown, so she read some more on how to do it. Eventually, it began to look as it should, with a light application of powder, a little bit of rouge (but only a little) and the same with eyeshadow and brown mascara. She chose a light-coloured lipstick and ran a brown pencil line on her now thinned out eyebrows. To her, the effect was perfect.

There was one more problem – it was the voice. It had never been a deep voice but it still sounded masculine.

Dr Miller gave her a list of names and she chose a speech therapist, completely dismissing any surgery. It didn't take long before Mary learnt to speak in a higher tone without sounding false and ridiculous. She would practise this every day until she did it without thinking.

Her pieces on politics sent to the newspaper continued. One day, she received a letter from the editor wanting to meet her with the view to employment. He could meet with her on Tuesday of the following week, three pm at the main office in Blight Street. If he didn't hear otherwise, he would assume she would be there.

That day in July was filled with terror for Mary. The confidence she had gained over the last few months now abandoned her. She had conferred with her doctor who said he had complete faith in her transformation and her abilities. He strongly advised her to keep the appointment.

And so it was that Mary was sitting on a chair in the hallway facing the glass panels of internal offices. There was a lot of activity, loud talking and typewriter keys being speedily punched one finger at a time by untrained journalists.

Alex Walker, the editor, seemed to come out of nowhere to greet her. He was a tall, rotund man. He wasn't wearing a jacket. His shirt was crumpled and his tie slightly off to the side of the collar.

'Alex Walker,' he said.

'Mary Taylor,' she replied, using her best feminine voice.

His handshake was firm and strong. Hers, deliberately limp. For the briefest of moments, he looked at her inquiringly, his forehead slightly crinkled. The moment passed in an instant and she was shown to his office.

His large desk was haphazardly piled with papers and other assorted bits of paper. Shelves all around the walls were heaving with books of every kind. He sat in a huge chair and lit a cigar, his ashtray already filled with discarded half smoked butts. He didn't bother to ask if she minded.

'I'm very impressed with your literary style. Your understanding of a subject and analytical talent is of a very high standard,' he said.

'Thank you,' said Mary, still at the height of nervousness.

'Where did you study? Do you have a diploma?' he asked.

'I have to be honest with you, Mr Walker, I haven't studied journalism. I write what I perceive to be the situation and I have read a great deal on many subjects since I was a child. Newspaper articles have been my preferred source since I can remember. I have some cuttings of opinion pieces I wrote while in New Zealand. I wrote them anonymously because, well, I suppose, I just wanted privacy.' Most of what she said was true.

'Frankly, I think it an advantage you haven't studied it.' He smiled, taking another puff of his cigar. 'Your mind is not set in the academia, if you know what I mean.' He then proceeded to read one of her opinion pieces. 'Well, excellent, excellent,' he commented, mainly to himself. 'Are you from New Zealand?'

'Yes,' said Mary.

He wasn't that interested about her birthplace so she didn't have to lie about anything else.

'Well, I would like to offer you a job here. Keep in mind you will be the only female in the office. Does that worry you?'

'Not at all,' replied Mary.

'Good. Right. Now to start with, it won't be politics you'll report on. I want reports on the social scene. All those so-called society parties and who attended – a bit of a who's who, if you like. Women also want to know what they were wearing, what's the latest fashion. Then I would like you to do an opinion piece about the ordinary woman who stays at home. Does she want to work? What jobs are available to women and how do women feel about unequal pay? For starters I will pay you two pound fifty a week plus travel costs. Do you have a car?'

'Not at the moment,' said Mary.

'Right, it's not essential at this stage but it's preferable.'

'I'll look into that straight away,' promised Mary.

'Right. When can you start?'

'Would next Monday be alright?'

'That will do nicely. We'll set up a desk, phone and typewriter for you.'

'Thank you, Mr Walker. I'm excited to be starting here.'

They shook hands and Mary departed, feeling as if she was floating out the door.

Chapter 20

In 1960 Rebecca and Tim started high school. Kathleen, as always, provided all Rebecca needed for her education.

The two young students found secondary school a bit confusing to start with. There were different teachers for different classes, for instance. There were time schedules and different classrooms for each subject. After a couple of weeks, they became familiar with how it worked and started to lap up all that secondary school offered. By all accounts this was a very good school and all pupils benefited from the subjects being taught and for the best of staff teaching them. One thing stood out – it was the encouragement to become independent thinkers and to take responsibility for homework, attendance and uniform.

Another new event took place in Hobart that year: television. It was not yet in their households but some of their friends had a set. Occasionally they were permitted to view a show on the weekend. It was an exciting time. Some pleading took place but it was quite a while before their own families relented.

By the time Rebecca and Tim were promoted to year five they had gained the reputation for being studious and responsible young adults who passed all chosen subjects very well indeed. Out of school times though, they played Beatles music. Both had record players and they, along with teenagers around the world, were swept up by this sensation. Parents and grandparents alike were worried and suspicious of this new scene. The group never promoted it but listening to them seemed to go hand-in-hand with smoking and drinking alcohol.

Bec and Timmy (as they were referred to by their peers) went along to a party held by a student friend whilst his parents were away for the weekend. They smoked a cigarette and drank some beer along with the others. Tim was sick outside and Rebecca wasn't far behind. It was a lesson they never forgot. Rebecca had a smoke now and then at any party they attended but Tim abstained from it altogether. It was the only time they argued. He disapproved of her smoking at all.

Kathleen was now fifty-nine years old and still working hard at the shop. She continued to miss Harold; he was the only man in her life and she would never re-marry. Her hair was starting to grey and a few wrinkles appeared around her eyes but her beauty remained.

Rebecca's father John had left two weeks after Harold's funeral. He wrote Lillian a note saying he didn't want this marriage anymore and said he was going to Launceston to start a new life. He took the car he had never paid off. He didn't apologise for that or anything else, for that matter. Lillian and Kathleen weren't surprised and Rebecca didn't care at all. Shortly after, Lillian and her daughter moved in with Kathleen and remained there.

Lillian had the occasional suitor. She loved going to dances with them and some seemed to be serious. But none lasted for long. They found Lillian too difficult – she would become possessive and jealous in these relationships and it turned men away from her.

Just after Rebecca's thirteenth birthday, Kathleen heard screams coming from her room. She rushed and opened the door to find Lillian hitting her daughter. This horrible occurrence made Kathleen so angry she pushed Lillian away so hard she nearly fell.

'If you ever, ever, hit this child again, I will put you out of this house for good. I mean it, for good. Do you understand?'

'Yes,' replied Lillian, meekly.

After that outburst she kept her resentment of her growing, beautiful daughter hidden. Rebecca had become used to her mother's unforgivable behaviour, she had ceased to care about her a long time ago. Kathleen more than made up for this lost relationship.

New products had been introduced to the grocery shop: frozen vegetables, takeaway prepared meals and a few cosmetic items such as hand and face creams. Hector made sure the business kept up with the times. Supermarkets were becoming established and he wanted to expand and be competitive. Most of the long-term, devoted customers remained with them. The nearest supermarket was too far away anyway. Besides, they liked being served and not to have to serve themselves.

They were nearing the end of their last year at high school. Tim had been elected prefect and Rebecca was very proud of him. They were both now seventeen. They were at Tim's place while his parents were away for the weekend, visiting Tim's uncle in Huonville. Rebecca was sitting with Tim on the top of his bed, talking, something they did often. They were making plans for the next stage of their lives. They were laughing and mucking about, punching each other and rolling around like a couple of lion cubs. Suddenly, they were still. Rebecca was lying on the bed and Tim found himself looking down at her. To him, she was always beautiful, but at that moment, he realised just how beautiful. He suddenly kissed her – it was an impulsive thing, but the next was much longer. Rebecca kissed him back.

Before they could speak, they were tearing at each other's clothes then Tim was inside her. It hurt her at first and Tim said sorry.

'It's alright,' she said.

It was the first time for both of them. It was quick and a bit awkward, but they giggled and were happy. Rebecca knew she was no longer a virgin. He apologised to her again.

'Don't apologise, I'm so glad it was you,' she said.

They made love again later that day.

From that day on, they made love often. Rebecca insisted on Tim wearing a condom. She had no intention of becoming pregnant. He didn't want that either. Through word of mouth, he found a doctor who strongly believed in family planning. His beliefs were not popular with others in his field but he gave Tim some condoms with no judgement attached.

It was in February 1966 that Rebecca and Tim went separate ways in their pursuit of further education. Tim to university in Sandy Bay to study optical engineering. His dream was to work on telescopes. Rebecca went to teacher's college in Hobart. Her dream was to teach English and bring the love of books to her pupils. They met up as often as possible and would walk together as always. Both had part-time jobs now.

Tim in a milk bar in Sandy Bay and Rebecca did waitressing at one of the cafés in Hobart. Between travelling to and from home, part-time work and studying, they didn't have much time to spend with each other. In 1967 both were offered scholarships, which lessened the financial burden for both their families, especially Kathleen.

Despite their consuming commitments, Rebecca and Tim made time to attend some of the parties held by friends from teacher's college and uni. The sixties were a time of immense change. Fashion was fluctuating and it was not unusual to see Rebecca wearing a mini skirt, coloured tights and white go-go boots along with teased long hair and a headband. It took Tim longer to embrace it but, eventually, he started wearing slim fit trousers and polo shirts. He now sported glasses but he refused to grow his hair. The uni gang thought him a bit of a nerd but it was their term of endearment for him. They knew he was a genius. To Rebecca he always looked decidedly sexy and he felt the same of her.

Among the group, a few men hung on to the bodgie and widgie era, wearing stove-peg pants with luminous ties and socks. Every dress code was accepted as the norm.

At these parties cigarette smoke hung in the air like a fog and, along with constant chatter, music played in the background. The Easybeats, The Beatles, Spicks and Specks and Billy Thorp and the Aztecs were among the favourites. No subject was off limits either. It ranged from the intellectual to gossip and the latest shows on TV. Of course, there was never-ending astonishment and discussion about space exploration. Tim especially found this to be a miracle of science and technology, which fed his enthusiasm for study into telescopes.

In this atmosphere of fun and laughter there would always be a moment of solemnity when Black Tuesday was relived. Everyone was touched by it. Either by the death of a relative, the burning of their homes or the sheer horror of that day, not to mention the near loss of the university. In the aftermath, many would reflect on how they conducted their lives while many suffered in silence.

Lillian was now forty. At times she was sweet and cooperative, at others sullen and uncommunicative. She helped out at the shop at intervals but in between she stayed in bed. Unlike other women, she hadn't moved with the times and still wore the same hairstyle, make-up and clothes. Kathleen was at a loss about what to do with her. The medical profession's only answer was to give her more tablets; she still refused to see a psychiatrist. Rebecca began to suspect her mother was addicted. She had once suggested this to Lillian who vehemently denied it.

'Frankly, Mum, you need to do something about yourself. You're addicted, admit it,' said Rebecca.

'Mind your own business. This is nothing to do with you,' Lillian replied angrily.

Rebecca shrugged her shoulders and walked away. *Why do I even try with you?* she thought.

One day Kathleen asked Rebecca to meet her at the café after she finished her shift. 'Keep it to yourself,' she said in a whisper.

Rebecca nodded.

On the appointed day Kathleen and her granddaughter sat together at a table located at the rear of the café. They each had a cup of tea and cake.

'Are you alright, Grandma? What did you want to talk about?'

'Now, you're not to worry. I want to talk about arrangements I've made for the future.'

'Is there anything wrong?'

'No, not at all,' said Kathleen reassuringly. 'I've made a will. I'm leaving the house to you.'

'I thought you would leave it to Mum.'

'Never. She's not capable. She would sell it and waste all the money. However, she can stay in it as long as she lives, unless she damages the house. Then you have every right to get her out.' Kathleen was emphatic about her plan.

'Grandma, I don't want to think about you not being around. I love you so much and I'm grateful for everything you have done for me.'

'I know you are, darling. Your grandpa and me will always love you too. He would be so proud, as proud as I am now. Promise me you will never sign over the house to your mother,' she pleaded.

'I promise,' said Rebecca, kissing her grandmother. 'You're going to be around forever anyway.'

'Hmmm,' Kathleen replied. 'One other thing: I have opened a bank account and nominated my solicitor and Hector joint signatories to it. When I'm no longer here they will manage the utility bills for the house. Lillian will give them to Hector and he will arrange payments and so on. She is not to have anything else from this account. She is perfectly capable of work. If she needs money for other things, she has to work for them. She has been getting child endowment for you but that only lasts until you're twenty-one.'

'Oh, I didn't know that,' said Rebecca, very surprised.

'We've had arguments about all that. As you know I have been supporting you, and I love to do it. But I didn't see why Lillian should keep it all to herself. She's been passing it on to me now. It's not a lot but it helps with your educational needs.'

'Sorry about all this, Grandma.'

'You don't have to be. It's your mother who needs to be sorry. You've had a tough time with her. Your father hasn't been any help either.'

'Grandma, you and Grandpa have cared for me and I have always felt loved. That is more than enough. Mum doesn't matter to me.'

'Alright … you've changed your hair and wearing shorter skirts now. Do you think that's wise?' she asked, changing the subject with a smile on her face.

'Don't worry, Grandma, I'm looking after myself.'

Kathleen put her hand on Rebecca's face and looked at her. 'Take care, child. I have to get back now.'

They hugged each other and Kathleen walked off towards the tram stop. Rebecca watched her. She had good posture and lovely legs but she noticed her walk was slower now. She felt so sad for her. Kathleen was sixty-two, living without her dear Harold, coping on her own.

At the end of 1968 Rebecca received her primary teacher qualification and Tim his diploma in engineering. He needed to stay another year and work towards his bachelor degree, while Rebecca would apply to primary schools for a position. Before that, they could happily spend time together.

Neither had officially celebrated this milestone with their families. So, Kathleen and Mabel decided to hold an afternoon tea for them both at Mabel and Richard's home. A few of their friends from their student days were invited too. Lillian exhibited the better side of her personality on that wonderful day. No one who attended was in any doubt that Tim and Rebecca would one day marry.

Chapter 21

1969 marked nearly seventeen years that Mary had worked for the newspaper. She had turned forty-seven. There were many personal changes for her. She had bought the Old Victorian Cottage in Cooper Street. Later she became an Australian citizen and had finally gained a passport as Mary Taylor in 1959. Both these applications were fraught with fear and worry, as she had to provide her previous birth and current change of name certificates. Her concern abated when nothing adverse came to the attention of immigration. Newspaper items that appeared in Tasmania and New Zealand, along with the 1952 police record, never surfaced, neither was she on any wanted list. Mary assumed they thought Cecil was dead.

She had also gained a driver's licence, brought a Volkswagen Beetle and wore expensive pantsuits and jewellery. She never wore a dress. Her colleagues had become used to her appearance and her presence, no longer whispering among themselves about who this woman was. Her work spoke for itself; she was highly respected. The now retired editor, Alex Walker, never had reason to regret his decision to hire her. In the midst of handing over to his successor, Mary was given the highest praise.

Mary worked hard to prove her worth. As required at the beginning of her employment she started reporting on the social scene. Her appointed photographer had a car and they would take off day or night to any event they knew was happening. It was not something she enjoyed. Usually, she would find most of the women at these events superficial and they found her an oddity, but this was in her favour. Their inability to put their finger on it, to define her, interested them and they invariably welcomed her, wanting to know more. Her clever interview style quickly turned attention away from their inquisitiveness and they were soon imparting details of their private lives. She would write her articulate descriptions of the architecture, atmosphere and intricate details about the dresses worn by the women. Always there was some titillation toward the end of the article but never their real names. It would be, 'Mrs X is getting a divorce; her marriage is over,' or, 'Mrs Z is in love with someone else but doesn't know how to tell her husband'.

Women read these articles voraciously. Mary also started a Dear Abby column answering questions about everyone's love lives. Not that she always knew what to say. If she didn't, she'd make it up.

Her next venture was to put an item in the paper about working conditions for women. She wanted to interview them and gave her work number for the purpose. Her phone didn't stop ringing. There were complaints of segregation in the work place. That is, women could only work in jobs defined by their sex: shop assistants, stenographers, clerks and so on, regardless of their qualifications. And there were always the comments such as, 'Well you'll end up getting pregnant and were does that leave us?' Many articles were written on this subject. In the end she had to stop taking calls, it was overwhelming.

One day the editor called her into the office. He wanted her to report on the Sydney to Hobart yacht race. Her flight and accommodation would be paid for. She said yes of course, but secretly the thought of going back to that place made her very apprehensive. She lost hours of sleep over it. She needn't have worried. No one recognised the former Cecil and she came back with some brilliant writing about the winner, Kurrewa IV, the crew and celebrations.

The trip was bittersweet. The escape from the wharf on that fateful day was still vivid, but was soon countered by triumph and the congratulations she received for her article.

After that she was given a desk in the sports department and wrote about rugby, golf and tennis. She stayed at that desk for the next few years.

In 1960 Mary was given another opportunity. She was appointed the foreign correspondent for the paper and her first post was London. Arrangements had to be made around her domestic life. She asked for her mail to be picked up. Any bills that needed to be paid in her absence would be covered by the paper. Her trusted doctor gave her a year's supply of estrogen with strict instructions that if she felt ill, she was to seek medical advice. Secure in the knowledge all details were now in good hands, she boarded a plane for the long journey to London. There were many stops on the route and it took approximately thirty-five hours.

She was met at the airport by one of the staff from the London paper for which she was grateful. They had obviously sent a junior on this errand because others were too busy to do it. He didn't seem to mind. His name was Peter and he was very chatty. His accent suggested he was well educated but it wasn't a plum-in-the-mouth kind of speech. His youthful enthusiasm was palpable. Accommodation had been organised and the building was situated a block from the paper's office. Mary's bags were carried inside to the foyer. She was to rest up and they would see her tomorrow at nine am.

'The office is just a block down from here on your left-hand side, you can't miss it,' Peter said. 'Have a good rest and see you then. Cheerio.' He disappeared before Mary could thank him.

After signing in she took the small cramped lift to her room. It was certainly small – she felt she could hardly turn around but it did have its own small bathroom with an electric shower. The single bed was against a wall and the cupboard for clothes was not very adequate but she managed. There was also a small table with one chair. *Be thankful*, she reminded herself.

After a long sleep and a good English breakfast, she walked the block to the Fleet Street office. This was a city alive with unrelenting activity. Looking up and around she felt dwarfed and in awe of the staggering amount of beautiful architecture and was hungry to learn the history behind it. She vowed to explore, to drink it in, savour it all.

She reached the office. It was a large, aged stone building. She was directed to the second floor. Mary opened the door and entered a room that resembled an explosion site. There were long tables where journalists sat at various angles on chairs, some talking loudly on a phone. People were at typewriters, papers were haphazardly dropped all over the place, a couple of telex machines rapidly tapped out messages. Men's jackets were casually placed in any space that was left. It was as if they had been there all night. The place was throbbing.

At the other end of the long room, a man came out of his office towards her. She knew it must be the editor – he had the same persona, rotund, crumpled shirt and crooked tie. She quietly smiled to herself.

'Hello. Can I help you?' he asked, with teeth that looked like they needed a bit of attention.

'Hello. I'm Mary Taylor, the journalist from Australia.'

'Oh, hello! Welcome to London,' he said with enthusiasm and vigorous handshaking. 'I'm Bert Hammond, the editor.'

For a brief second, he gave her that indiscernible look – she was used to it.

'How are you feeling? It's a very tiring journey I'm told. I've always dreamt of seeing Australia, bit long in the tooth now probably. Anyway, let me make a space for you,' he said while steering her to a corner in the room. 'We have a spare typewriter. I'm sure you'll find everything you need, if not just ask. You can hang your coat over there if you want … um… You can make yourself a cuppa over there and um … We usually have a drink at the local after work, come and join us. Alright? Um … Take your time, have a look around, get the feel, so to speak, ask as many questions as you like and um … I'll see you shortly.' Bert looked decidedly tired while at the same time radiating energy.

Mary hung up her coat and sat down at the typewriter. She shook hands with some who quickly introduced themselves. After a moment she rose, made a cup of tea then started to scan newspapers that were scattered around, reading everything that was happening in London. She had her steno pad and pens with her and began making notes.

After work she walked with Bert and other journalists to the local pub. It was crowded to bursting with others in the same profession. The noise inside was rowdy and boisterous, making it almost impossible to hear each other. If others spoke to her, she would nod in agreement, hoping it was the right response. Most of the time Bert was beside her. She summed him up as being a very overworked man with a boundless generosity of spirit. She liked him. As it was too hard to hold a conversation she leant back on the bar and just enjoyed the atmosphere. It was exhilarating.

Next day Mary sent a telex message to her editor, confirmed her accommodation, thanked him again for sending her and gave him an idea of when to expect her first article. She wanted to write about the UK parliament first. Bert helped her with directions and showed her where to catch the underground. It was a short walk to Temple Station, a very short train trip and another short walk to the Houses of Parliament. She knew it was a sitting day and had a journalist ID just to make sure she had entry. It was very exciting to be sitting in the gallery and listing to the debates. Harold Macmillan was prime minister and Mary felt like a child who had just experienced their very first ride on a merry-go-round. What surprised her was the nonstop shouting and bobbing up and down of the ministers, seeking the attention of the speaker. The Australian Parliament seemed sedate compared to this rabble. She was captivated. Time seemed to flash by and she had to leave. Her intention was to now see Westminster. Seeing the Abbey took her breath away. She looked around at this beautiful, glorious structure with wonder and emotion. On her way out she grabbed a pamphlet about the Abbey and caught a train back to Temple Station.

On arrival at the office, she typed a piece about the House of Commons, then a piece about Westminster Abbey and its history and sent it off with a stock photo of the church. Telexes were a new innovation and the process was slow but it was better than nothing. She reminded herself to purchase a camera.

Some of her reports were about the disturbances in London, especially by its younger people. There was talk of a bohemian underground movement whose members were anti-establishment and taking drugs. While she was unable to gain access to this group, she did seek answers from many who had been involved and who subsequently discarded the whole concept, either from disillusionment or fear they would die young from all the unknown drugs offered. She gained this knowledge simply by hitting the pubs and asking questions while assuring them their names would never be revealed. People always trusted her, like the society women back in Australia. Her way of gaining trust and finding out the truth was becoming legendary amongst the other journalists.

There were also many protests against the Vietnam War, even though Britain had not sent in troops. There were whispers about unofficial help from Britain for training though, and that was enough for the young anti-establishment crowd to bring out their placards and march in the streets.

Mary also provided news about the fashion scene along with photos, thinking women would like to see the latest, and she was right.

Her spare time was spent travelling around London admiring buildings, pubs and spending hours in museums and art galleries, some of which she also wrote about, along with the changing of the guard at Buckingham Palace. Photos were regularly sent too, taken with her newly acquired camera.

At the end of twelve months she was recalled home. Saying goodbye to everyone was hard, she was especially despondent about leaving Bert. He always found time to give her advice and support, despite his heavy schedule. She hugged him, keeping a space between their bodies, just in case he could tell. Even though she had developed small breasts and her genitals had shrunk, she wasn't about to take chances.

Bert decided he wanted to take her to the airport. On the drive they were making small talk.

'You're the best foreign journalist we've had, you know,' he said.

Mary smiled.

'You must be aware there's been talk about you. Some don't know what to make of you. I suspect you've had something done to yourself and, frankly, I don't care, it's none of my business. What I want to say is never let prejudice get in the way of your talent. Keep doing what you're doing with confidence and commitment. Your reporting style is unique. I think one day you'll be recognised for it. I do,' he said with conviction and a wide grin.

They had arrived at the airport. He gathered up her luggage and took her inside. He gave her a kiss on the cheek and said, 'Good luck to you.' He walked away, looked back once, then he was gone. She stood there, alone, with tears running down her face. No one had ever been that kind to her.

She found a note in the letterbox when she arrived back and along with her house key there was a card saying welcome home from Brian, the editor. Her emotions came to the surface again. She felt drained and tired.

Someone had put some food in the fridge for her. This final thoughtful act sent her into an hour of weeping.

It was early 1961. Her first day back in the office was met with congratulations from everyone and a talk with Brian. He again thanked her for all her work and how much he admired her mental acuity. Paper distribution had increased as a result of her opinions on UK politics and other reports she had written. They had gained more women readers as well. He advised she was to have a rest for the moment; they would talk about another assignment later. She expressed her thanks to him and all the others. 'Who put all that delicious, fattening food in my fridge?'

They all put up their hands and everyone laughed.

Her doctor called her in for a checkup of her liver and cholesterol levels.

'Your health is quite good, but your blood pressure is a bit high. You need a bit of rest,' he said.

'Alright, I'll ask the boss for a couple of days.' Mary was given those days and more if she needed.

A Sydney summer can be humid and one day Mary decided to cool off at the beach. She had no intention of wearing a swimsuit and would never swim again. But she did have a pair of shorts that reached the knee and wore them with a short blouse over a thin singlet. It was a joy to be walking along the edge of the sand, splashing her feet and feeling the breeze.

The beach was crowded with singles, couples and people with children. It was joyful seeing parents introduce their children to the water for the first time. Most loved it; a few ran from it as fast as they could.

Mary's mother inexplicably came to mind. She hadn't thought about her for years. She recollected desperately needing her after her father had given a beating for something trivial; but she never intervened, never supported her young child or berated her husband for his actions. There was no forgiveness then, and Mary didn't forgive them now.

Soon there was another assignment – this time to Canberra for six months, another short stint in Sydney then to Japan. That assignment would create controversy. There were many soldiers who would never forget the unspeakable horror of the Japanese labour camps and inhumane treatment of the men. Rather than revive the memory of those horrendous acts, she focused on peace and wrote about the Hiroshima Peace Memorial Museum and the sicknesses and disfigurement inflicted on the Japanese people caused by the bomb. Along with those articles, she wrote about the population and rebuilding of Japan. Her accounts touched many and enraged others.

In her capacity as the foreign correspondent, she visited many countries and cities, some more than once, including London. Bert had retired but they caught up for drinks. He looked tired and didn't seem well but his capacity for a laugh, his joy of life and a drink hadn't diminished. His wife had died but he did have grown up children who he was close to.

'Do you have someone?' he asked.

'Nope, don't want one,' said Mary. 'Why? Are you offering?' she said with a grin.

'No, but if I was in Australia, we would be good mates, as you Aussies say,' he said, giving her a quick squeeze.

She was in the company of a kind, understanding human being; she wished she could take him back with her.

Mary also covered the fires in Hobart, February 1967. This time she had no qualms in going. A photographer came with her and took many photos of this horrific fire. Both these professionals abstained from recording some images; they didn't want to invade people's privacy during their most defenseless time. The devastation was enormous. People died, acres of land and homes were completely destroyed, sheep and cattle lost as well as farms, along with any foreseeable income. They couldn't speak on their way home to Sydney.

It was at this time that interstate reporting became easier with the introduction of the facsimile. All journalists, including Mary, made use of this new technology with gusto.

It was a warm, frenetic day at the paper when, suddenly, there was a thud. For a split second everyone was fixed in their positions, unable to move. Mary had dropped to the floor. Brian was the first to rush to her.

'She's unconscious. Call an ambulance quickly.'

Someone picked up a phone, someone loosened her blouse, someone took off her shoes, someone brought her some water and someone put a wet handkerchief to her forehead.

The ambulance arrived. She was still unconscious and taken straight to hospital.

Mary woke up slowly. She became aware of a needle in her hand with a tube leading to an IV drip. A jug of water and a glass stood on a metal cabinet beside the bed. She could hear voices but could see nothing beyond the bed. The clean white sheets made a rustling sound with her every move. Lifting them up confirmed her worst fears. Her clothes had been removed, replaced with a medical gown. *Oh, God!* she thought. *They know.* She lay there thinking for a moment. What would their response be? Panic like this hadn't visited her for years.

The curtain that encircled the bed parted slightly and a nurse entered.

'Hello, there,' she said, with a bright, cheery voice. 'I'm Sister Rosalind. Everyone calls me Rosy. How are you feeling? You gave us a bit of a fright there.'

Mary's wrist was efficiently picked up and a thermometer placed in her mouth before she could answer. Sister Rosy looked at her watch while counting her pulse then she entered something on a chart hanging from the end of the bed. The examination, done in silence, was methodical.

'Well, all that seems good. There's some water there if you need it. Just sip slowly. Doctor will be with you shortly then you can have something to eat.' Sister Rosy was out through the curtain before Mary could utter a word.

Tiredness descended. Despite her worry she nodded off. A doctor arrived and woke her up an hour later.

'Hello, Mary. How are you now? Do you feel dizzy? Weak?' he asked, shining a pencil light into one eye after another.

'I feel tired,' Mary replied.

'Yes, well you would, your blood pressure dropped. It was dangerously low when you came in. You'll need to stay here overnight for observation. What medications are you taking?'

'Sorry, I don't know your name.'

'Oh, of course, my apologies. Dr Moore. I'm the emergency doctor here.'

He seemed pleasant but Mary didn't know where to start. She remained close-mouthed.

'I can see you're worried, Mary, but don't be. While you're here you are my patient and everything is strictly confidential. The nursing staff are very discreet, I promise you. Myself and Sister Rosalind will be the only people looking after you. And just so you know, we are certainly not judgmental. Now, I assume you are taking estrogen and a testosterone block, would that be correct?'

'Yes,' said Mary.

'Right. Could you give me your doctor's name and contact number, please? I'll contact him to let him know what's happened and confirm what you're taking. He might want to change it or lower the dose. In the meantime, I suggest you rest and, don't worry, we'll look after you. I'm a big fan of your articles by the way.'

Tears of relief rolled slowly down to her chin. She thought of Pat again, as she did every day, then she slept.

On her release from hospital, Mary was given a letter for Dr Miller with advice to see him as soon as possible. The doctor advised she look after herself, wished her the best of luck and said goodbye.

She made a phone call and was able to see Dr Miller later in the day. Dr Miller remained her anchor and support through everything.

'That must have rocked your confidence. Are you feeling alright now? Dr Moore has given you a clean bill of health.'

'Yes, I'm fine. That's never happened before, it was frightening. They had also put me in a hospital gown. I was mortified.'

'I understand your fears but you need never worry. Both Dr Moore and the sister who attended you espouse the rights of people to change gender, should that be their wish.'

Mary nodded in agreement.

'I've adjusted your medication and had my staff get it for you. I understand it's still a bit problematic, picking it up yourself, especially given you are rather famous now,' he said with a smile.

'Thank you, Doctor, I appreciate your understanding.'

'Quite alright, that's my job … Uh … I want to ask you something. It will stay in this room of course.'

'Go ahead,' said Mary.

'Well, there is absolutely no doubt of your conviction to change gender and your readiness for it, none at all. But I've always thought there was also a catalyst that spurred you on. Just a hunch. Were you running away from something that happened in New Zealand? Look, I only ask to check your mental health. If it was a calamitous event, it may not have gone away, despite your change. I want to make sure you're not suffering depression or other problems that can affect your mental stability. I only ask for your sake.'

Mary was already feeling a bit down and tempted, as never before, to reveal everything. After a long pause she said, 'You're very perceptive, Doctor. I was running away from my father, as far as I could. He had given me a large share of money he received from the sale of his sheep station. He said he wanted me to make a man of myself. What he really meant was get out of my sight and never come back.' All this was true.

'I'm so sorry.' Dr Miller was genuinely sympathetic.

'It's quite alright. I'm happier than I've ever been. I've made a new life – a good part of that is due to you. While my childhood was not ideal, I've come to terms with it, long ago. I'm not depressed.' Another true statement.

'That's good to know. Well, if that's all, I have someone waiting.'

'Of course, thank you again for everything,' said Mary with gratitude.

They shook hands.

When back home she called the office. They insisted she take two weeks off. Reluctantly, she accepted.

She decided she would buy a television. It was installed two days later and she couldn't stop watching this new, novel distraction.

Mary witnessed many changes in the office. Word processors were in use now and later PCs. Along with better functioning facsimiles, there were also photocopiers. All of these innovations improved the speed of output by journalists. She welcomed all of it.

Among writing articles about the local political scene, she continued travelling as their foreign correspondent until 1982, when travelling became too tiring. The paper offered her the position of editor, but she declined. After observing the toll it took on the health of past editors, she was not persuaded.

In 1987 Mary had reached the age of sixty-five. Although she wasn't pushed in any way, she chose to retire. She had enough. The farewells seemed to go on for longer than expected. There were speeches and accolades, TV news items about her career, many catch-ups in pubs from others working in the same field, a gift of a very expensive watch from the paper along with free daily papers for the rest her life and a personal letter from a government minister.

On her final day, she cleaned her desk, gathered up her personal items, which included many photos, said a final, tearful goodbye and left the paper for good.

She drove home and although sad for the end of an era, she had an exhilarating feeling of freedom. She had plenty of money in the bank, including the balance of what was left from her father's money. Her spending was still frugal; there were no concerns about surviving comfortably for a long time. She was eligible for the pension and she would eventually apply. But before that, she had made a decision. Another move. Sydney had become too fast and busy. Besides, she never got used to the humidity, which sucked all her energy, or the ever-present threat of being bitten by a funnel web. Melbourne was her preference. During her few visits there she became impressed by its gardens, buildings and its seemingly milder weather.

But first, there was much to do, mainly the selling of her house in Cooper Street. She looked up housing prices for the area and engaged an estate agent. She discussed agent fees, bringing them down a little. She was convinced her sale price was correct as it included all the furniture and white goods along with a TV. A few buyers were interested. It took a month, but finally, after adjusting her price down by two thousand dollars, it was sold. Despite the age of her house, she had looked after it and had made a profit.

Next, she traded in her very loved Volkswagen Beetle and purchased a new Honda Accord Hatchback. She gave her beetle a long look before she drove off. It made her cry. She felt silly but couldn't help it.

The remaining days were spent cramming the new car with her personal belongings. She was ready to go before the thirty days were up. She drove to the estate agents office and handed over the keys, thanked him and drove out of Sydney for the last time.

It was estimated it would take at least ten to twelve hours to get to Melbourne via the Hume Highway. She began her journey early on a Thursday morning. The first stop was Holbrook, a town located halfway to Melbourne. After an overnight stay she determined to keep going straight on. Leaving at seven am, with one toilet stop and a quick lunch, she finally arrived in Melbourne at three-thirty pm, booked into a motel not far from the city centre and rested.

She made an appointment with an estate agent, situated in a place of interest. After arriving about three quarters of an hour later, Mary and the agent, Mr Stuart, were shaking hands.

'How was your drive down?' he asked.

'Very good, thank you. Better than expected.'

'Good, good. Well, let's go and have a look at a couple of houses I think may interest you,' he said. 'What made you decide to come to Melbourne?' Mr Stuart asked, while driving fast and unpredictably.

'The weather and the gardens,' said Mary, who was becoming increasingly tense with his driving.

'Alright, here we are. I have two to show you – this is the first one.'

He pulled up sharply in front of a small, newly painted weatherboard. It had a picket fence and a neat garden. Inside were two bedrooms, a small kitchen, a dining area, bathroom and toilet. There was a small deck leading to the backyard that was neatly mown with a few eucalypts scattered around but no garden to speak of. It didn't exactly enthuse her.

'Right, let's go to the next one, shall we?' he said.

At this stage Mary made no comment one way or the other.

The next house was two streets away from the main road. It was a brick dwelling, slightly larger than the previous house. The front garden was all mowed grass and tall trees, with a path to the front door. It was tidy, without looking manicured. She loved it. The front door had a stained-glass panel inserted at the top. The opened door revealed a sealed, light timber hallway. On either side were the bedrooms and the walls were white. Further down the hallway revealed a pleasant surprise, a large open space with bifold glass doors filling the entire width of the back wall, opening onto a deck of equal length. There were native trees and bushes in the crowded back yard, with paving stones placed between and a neglected vegetable garden near the rear fence.

With her back to the garden, she stood still while her eyes wandered around the room. It comprised of a large, light coloured leather lounge surrounded by odd-sized comfortable chairs and a Coonara heater set into the brick wall off to the side. Nothing matched but it looked proportioned and welcoming. On the other side stood a country-style kitchen accompanied by a long kitchen bench. A door set back, past the kitchen, opened to a small sunroom with the bathroom and toilet at the end.

Mary instinctively knew this was where she wanted to be.

'Why are the owners selling?' asked Mary.

'I'm afraid there has been a tragedy. The owners died in an accident while on an overseas trip. Their children now live interstate. They want to sell it and the contents, if you want them, as soon as possible.'

'Can we go back and discuss it?' said Mary.

'Certainly.'

The drive back was just as harrowing but the office wasn't too far away, fortunately. They talked about price and details for an hour. Mary wanted to keep the furniture and, for the first time in her buying life, didn't barter. Documents were filled out and signed and the cheque made out. They shook hands and parted. Mary was as happy as a person with a hidden burden could be.

Chapter 22

Kathleen had to drag Lillian to the shop with her every day, threatening the withdrawal of the cash she often gave her. Having to constantly deal with her intransigent daughter was taking its toll on Kathleen. Hector was concerned about her.

It was early January 1969 when Rebecca commenced applying to a few primary schools for a teaching position. It entailed some long interviews in front of a board of three serious-looking people. Rebecca's confidence wavered during some of these probing discussions. She came away thinking she had no hope.

One of the schools Rebecca applied for was one she had attended as a child. Two weeks later, Rebecca was helping her mother clean the house. The headmistress from that school called, asking if she could come in tomorrow for a 'chat', as she put it.

With some trepidation, Rebecca was waiting in her office, looking out the window and reminiscing about the happy days she spent in the playground. The headmistress came rushing in.

'Sorry to keep you, I was held up. Anne Johnson, pleased to meet you.'

It had been some time and she looked older but her smile was unmistakable.

'Oh goodness, I can't believe it … You're Anne Johnson.'

'Yes,' said Anne, bewildered.

'Oh, sorry. You won't remember me but I remember you.'

'Have we met?' asked Anne.

'It was a long time ago; I was five. My grandmother brought me to the kindergarten. She was anxious for me to start right then, I think. It was too late in the year for that though. However, you said I could come for a couple of sessions then register for the full sessions the following year.

My grandmother often said you were very kind.'

Anne looked at her then she picked up a slip of paper from her desk and read it.

'Rebecca Parke.' 'You're that Rebecca, granddaughter of the Whitman's?'

'Yes.'

'Please, please sit down.' She directed Rebecca to a chair. Anne sat down at her desk. 'I remember that moment. I'm so sorry about your aunt. It was a terrible loss. She obviously meant a lot to you.'

'Yes, she did, very much,' replied Rebecca.

After a moment of a painful memory, Anne changed the mood in the room with her smile and said, 'You did extremely well in your interview and have the credentials we are seeking. We would like to offer you the position of primary teacher at this school. Congratulations.'

This took Rebecca by surprise; she could hardly contain herself but she held back her exuberance, told herself to stay calm.

'Thank you, Miss Johnson. I have dreamed of becoming a teacher ever since I can remember. And I love this school – I used to be a pupil here.'

'Well, this is a day of coincidences.' Anne was pleased to discover she was giving this once sad child another opportunity. She handed Rebecca a folder. 'This contains the curriculum and other important information. You will be starting with the grade ones. Myself and all the teachers will meet a day before the school commences. After that I'd like to meet you all after school on Fridays. I also invite any teacher to see me at any time if they need to. We sometimes have the odd child who is having difficulties that need to be discussed. If it can't be resolved, parents are asked to come in as well.

'Right, well, I expect you would like to see your classroom and other parts of the school. There have been a few improvements since you were here, but in the main, it's the same.'

Some rooms and parts of the structure had been refurbished but Anne was right, it was still the same. Rebecca was also shown the staff room, a place where all children at one time or another had wondered what went on behind that closed door. It was pleasing to see the children's toilets and washbasins had been updated. She used to hate going to the toilet at school and would hold on until she got back to the shop if she could; but it wasn't always possible and she would have to go to that damp place with its cold seats and spend the shortest time her bladder would allow.

After inspecting the school and saying goodbye to Miss Johnson, Rebecca walked quickly across the school sports ground and up the street towards the shop. She looked up to the clouds and thanked her grandfather. She may not have believed in a god but she was sure Harold was looking down on her and had something to do with her appointment.

By the time she reached the shop, she was almost breathless. She went straight to Kathleen and told her all that had happened. Lillian stood by and listened.

'That is wonderful, darling. You worked so hard, you deserve it. And at the same school you went to and, with Miss Johnson – I can't believe it,' she said, while hugging Rebecca tightly.

'Neither can I. What do you think, Mum?'

'Very good,' said Lillian, giving Rebecca an unemotional, light pat on her arm.

'Well done, Bec,' said Hector, who gave her a pat on the back and a kiss on the cheek.

Then she went to Tim's house and told him everything about the day in every detail.

'You're really something,' he said to Rebecca, giving her one of his delicious kisses. They hugged and cradled each other for a few minutes. Even though they hadn't said it, they loved each other deeply.

School started on the last day in January. Rebecca was nervous on her first day but it soon dissolved. All the children were happy to be at school, see their friends and eager to learn. They said, 'Good morning, Miss Parke,' and each said goodbye to her at the end of the day. She taught them the alphabet and times tables and read to them – her most favourite duty as their teacher.

It was late February. Tim and Rebecca were at a newly opened bistro. They'd finished the main course and were sipping their mixed drinks.

'I have something to tell you,' said Tim, sounding serious.

'What?' asked Rebecca, in her typically casual manner.

'I've been offered another scholarship.'

'That's fantastic. You're so clever,' she said, leaning across the table and giving him a kiss. She was feeling joyful and a little affected by her drink.

'It's serious.'

'What do you mean?'

'Um … It's with the University of Adelaide.'

'What?' said Rebecca, a little too loudly. She was suddenly sober.

'They kinda think I'm pretty good in my field and, well, they offered me a place. I don't want to leave you, Bec, but it's only for a year. It will certainly be advantageous for a future career in optical engineering. They have a lot to offer towards my studies. I've been thinking about it over the last few days and decided to accept. Please don't be angry.'

'I'm not angry, Tim, I'm just incredibly sad. How will I get on without you? I'm selfish, I know, but …' She trailed off.

'Look, we can see each other in the semester break or during the school holidays, if they happen at the same time. You can fly up or I can fly down, we'll figure it out. You know I'll miss you like hell, you must know that.'

She nodded but hung her head to hide her distress and the tears welling up.

They caught a taxi and, even though his parents were home asleep, he took her into his bedroom and quietly made love to her. Later they slipped out and he walked her back home. There were no lights on inside. He held her while they were standing by the front gate.

'I love you,' he whispered.

'And I love you,' she whispered back.

She watched him walk back up the empty street. He turned and waved a couple of times then he turned the corner and was out of sight.

During the next few days Rebecca tried to cheer up by telling herself it was only for a year. Besides, they could see each other in between.

The day came for him to leave. His parents drove him to the airport, taking Rebecca with them. After hugging and wishing him well, they retreated so Tim and Rebecca could have a private moment. They hugged each other very tightly, then kissed, then slowly let go. He walked towards the stewardess checking the boarding tickets, blew them all a kiss, waved and boarded the plane.

They stood at the viewing area and watched the aircraft until it was out of sight.

Mabel sat in the back seat of the car with Rebecca. They held hands, each staying strong for the other on the journey home. But once there, Rebecca broke down. Kathleen sat bedside her on the bed, offering words of comfort. Lillian brought her a cup of tea.

Teaching kept her occupied for which she was grateful. Being in charge of growing minds was to her a responsibility she took seriously. She loved being with her little pupils and they adored her. Their parents were equally enamored. Her female colleagues made sure she wasn't alone either. Some would take her out for a drive, or the pictures, some would go with her to the bistro, some would play tennis with her. One decided to teach her to drive. After a few weeks of gear crunching, laughter and some near misses with reverse parking, she was ready for her test.

She made one mistake. While doing a handbrake start, the engine stopped. She was asked to do it again and the second time, with a bit of a jerk, she did. Then she was off. The retired policeman who provided these tests ignored the not-so-perfect reverse parking and gave her a pass. He was a practical man and could tell someone who would improve with practise and those who needed to repeat the test, some more than once. Her teacher friends took her out to celebrate.

Tim called a couple of times, usually later in the evening when the communal phone in the hall wasn't in use. They had long talks on the phone but they couldn't do it very often. And they exchanged intimate letters, which they kept in secret places so they could read them again. She didn't tell him about her licence. She wanted to surprise him when he came back.

In the middle of June they both had a week of leave that coincided. Tim would fly down. Rebecca had purchased a second-hand car, a blue Hillman Minx. It was in good condition and hadn't done many miles. The owner had been transferred to an overseas posting. Hector, who knew something about cars, had come with her to see it. He did a bit of tyre kicking, engine inspection and revving. The interior was cream, as was the steering wheel. Only the driver's seat looked like a bottom had sat on it.

Hector whispered to her, 'Buy it, it's a good car. Beat down the price a bit though.'

She did as she was told and said she would buy it but could only afford two hundred and twenty-five dollars. There was some humming and harring but finally they agreed to two hundred and thirty dollars. This was most of Rebecca's savings but to her it was worth it. She showed him her licence details and gave him a cheque. He would have preferred cash. Hector spoke up for her honesty and said he could come back to the shop if it bounced. Rebecca followed Hector back in her car with the radio on. She was ecstatic.

The plane had finally landed. Rebecca placed herself in a position where she could see Tim emerge, barely able to contain her excitement. As soon as he came through, he went straight to her, kissed and hugged her and told her how much he had missed her.

'Where's Mum and Dad?'

'There's a surprise outside. Come on, let's get your bag first.'

Not questioning her further he grabbed her hand. 'You've done something to your hair,' he said.

'What do you think?'

'You are so beautiful,' he replied

He picked up his bag and they walked hand-in-hand towards her car.

'Surprise!'

'What?' he said, still not realising.

'I have a licence and this is my car,' she said triumphantly.

'Really? You drive and this is your car? Well, I'll be … That is amazing. You are amazing.' He picked her up a twirled her around.

'Come on,' she said. 'Your mum and dad are waiting for you. Everyone is there. Your uncle, grandma, mum, Hector and his family and some of the uni gang. Oh, and a couple of my friends from the school. Don't worry – we'll have time to ourselves. I've booked a place for us to stay later.'

He was smiling broadly while she was driving. He thought she was the most wonderful woman on earth, clever and beautiful. He loved her more than anything. He had brought a small engagement ring with him. He didn't have much money so it was a simple one but he wanted to ask her to marry him. Something more expensive would come later.

There were cheers from everyone when he walked in the door. There were streamers and balloons. A welcome home message had been iced onto a large cake that was sitting in the middle of the table. Around it was a variety of other smaller cakes, pastries and sandwiches. Everyone had contributed a plate of something they made. The long dining table was full and so was Tim's heart. He'd only been away for less than six months yet they were showing him how much he was missed and loved.

Music played, along with happy conversation, much laughter, dancing and eating. The house was buzzing. It continued to well into the night. By eleven pm the family was cleaning up.

'Tim and I are staying in the city tonight,' Rebecca announced out of nowhere. She was expecting a protest. Despite the so-called swinging sixties, this was still a conservative family.

Mabel was the first to speak. 'You are both sensible adults, you can do as you wish. Just remember we all care about you. Go and have your time together.' She turned back to the washing up. It seemed she spoke for everyone. No one else said a word.

Rebecca had her case already in her car. Tim grabbed a couple of things and the family kissed them goodbye with a, 'We'll see you tomorrow'. And they were on their way.

They arrived at Hadley's Hotel. Rebecca had booked a room in the name of Mr and Mrs Parke. As soon as they were in the room, they took off their clothes and made love more passionately than before. Afterwards, they were sitting up talking about anything and everything. Tim reached down over the side of the bed and fumbled inside a pocket of his abandoned jacket. He came back up with something in his hand.

'Bec,' he said seriously.

'What?' said Rebecca, giggling.

He opened the little box. 'Will you marry me?'

'Oh Tim, oh Tim. Yes, yes, yes!'

He put the ring on her finger. They kissed each other over and over and made love again.

They checked out late the next morning and headed for Tim's parents' house where they announced their engagement. There were squeals, congratulations, hugs and a pat on the back from his father.

'I just knew you were up to something,' said Mabel, even though it came as a surprise to Rebecca.

Then they walked hand-in-hand to the shop where they announced it again to Kathleen, her mother and Hector. Kathleen started crying, Hector kissed Rebecca on the cheek and, with a smile on his face, patted Tim on the back. Lillian gave them both a restrained hug and a kiss on the cheek, which was unusual for her.

Some happy days were spent together. Drives to the country and the beach, walks and the company of friends. Time passed so quickly. Before they knew it, they were at the airport saying goodbye again. On the way they had talked about how they felt, future plans and how they would miss each other. He promised he would ring and write as often as he could and reminded her it was only for a few more months. He turned, waved and smiled before he boarded. Rebecca cried while driving home.

Chapter 23

Mary discovered many benefits in living where she was. There were a couple of doctor's surgeries. She had visited one of them and found a good doctor, who, after reading Dr Miller's letter, was happy to give her what she needed. Eventually, she became confident enough to obtain her medication from the chemist in person. Still, she wore a scarf and glasses when doing so, as a precaution. There was also a food market, a butcher, a couple of gift shops and a train station. Sometimes, if the weather was warm, she would walk there and back.

Over the years she made many friends in the community. As well as helping raise funds for worthy causes, she opened her house for afternoon teas and gave parties that were legendary. Some knew her from her journalist days at the Sydney paper and considered her intelligent and eloquent. And, of course, she had many stories to tell, gained from her world travels. They all knew there was something different about her but instead of finding her odd, they thought her just a little eccentric, a title she enjoyed.

Mary and her next-door neighbour, Madge, were about the same age. Over time they had become good friends and enjoyed each other's company – they simply got on. It was purely a close friendship, which they both needed. There were drives to the countryside, walks to the shops, watching television or discussing the latest book they had read. Sometimes they caught a train to the city to see a film or buy clothing.

Madge had acquired a West Highland White Terrier, a lovely, biddable little female who was only ten months old. She adored it. It went everywhere with her. Mary, who had never had a pet, found her endearing.

It was about this time Mary turned seventy. Many people came to celebrate with her, some coming and going and some staying until late in the evening. It was a memorable day. She was starting to feel her age; there was a knee problem and she was starting to lose some of her hair. The doctor told her she might have osteoporosis. She wasn't concerned, just annoyed at the indications of old age when in fact she felt well and happy. She didn't want to know about it.

Marge came barging in Mary's front door one day, looking pale and worried.

'I have to have a heart operation.'

'What did they say?' asked Mary.

'I have a blocked valve.'

'Don't worry. You'll be fine. Surgeries of this kind have improved now, you'll get better.' She tried to comfort Madge and not show her own concern.

'Could you look after Darling while I'm in hospital?' She asked. Darling was the name she gave her dog.

'Of course, of course I will and I'll take you to the hospital.'

'Oh, thank you.'

Next morning Mary drove Madge to the hospital. She left her contact number with them and drove back home to look after Darling. Later that evening the hospital called to say Madge had died during the operation. Mary was devastated. She held the little terrier close to her and cried for hours. Madge was very dear to her. This loss of her valued friend was immeasurable.

There was a funeral the following week and Mary brought Darling with her. Many people attended. It was a sorrowful, gray, rainy day.

Madge had willed her money from the sale of the house, along with her savings, to the RSPCA, which was a fitting donation. She had chosen Darling from a group of pups that had been dumped there.

A young couple with a child eventually bought the house and, though they were good neighbours, it was not the same relationship Mary had had with Madge.

Two years later Mary was walking back from the supermarket with her shopping trolley and Darling on a lead. She was on the bitumen walking track used by runners, walkers and bike riders. The smooth surface cushioned Mary's sore feet.

It was a mild warm day; the breeze was washing over her face, she was enjoying the rare quiet moment on the path, not a person in sight. A large flock of corellas had just landed and were constantly chattering while picking seeds from the grass.

She was deep in thought, feeling contented with herself. Paper sales had tripled because of her, the community here benefited from her celebrity and her money. She was now who she had always wanted to be, there was honesty in that. Thoughts of Pat were rare, if at all. Mary had reached a kind of amity in her life.

Then, she dropped to the ground, her fall just missing Darling. The frightened dog was trying to escape but her lead was stuck underneath Mary who was now unconscious.

Finally, Darling grew exhausted and sat down beside her owner.

Chapter 24

It was the second half of 1969. School had resumed and Rebecca was back with her pupils. She was a conscientious, attentive teacher and colleague. This focused involvement also served to keep her from missing her dear Tim too much. They still communicated with each other regularly and he always finished with, 'It won't be long now, darling'.

The school year was coming to an end; time to start writing reports for the parents. Rebecca was very happy about all her pupils. They had different personalities, some were a bit smarter than others but they had one thing in common – they loved to learn and play. She hoped the joy of learning would continue throughout their lives.

The children were sitting at their desks drawing anything they wanted. Some were drawing the man on the moon, or their family, or the beach, or flowers, birds, trees and the sun.

Miss Johnson came into the room. She looked concerned.

'Rebecca, there are some policemen in my office who wish to speak with you,' whispered Miss Johnson.

'Oh! What about?'

'You need to go and see them, dear. I'll look after the children.'

They've found Cecil, she thought. *At last he can be brought to justice.*

Two police were waiting in the office. They had their caps off.

'Good afternoon. I'm Rebecca Parke. What is this about?'

'Good afternoon. This is Constable Hall and I am Sgt Davis.' They looked serious. 'We're very sorry to have to tell you this. Your fiancé, Tim Henderson, was killed in an accident.'

'What? That can't be right, you can't be right, I just spoke with him yesterday, he …' Rebecca put her hands to her face. 'Please, please … you are mistaken, you must be mistaken,' she implored them. Her whole body felt weak, she could hardly stand.

'We're very sorry, Miss Parke. We're sure it's Mr Henderson.'

'What happened?'

'He was crossing the road near the university. A large truck came around the corner, didn't see him and ran him down.'

'Oh no … this is wrong, this is wrong, this can't be happening.' She bent down, crying. 'Why? Why?'

Sgt Davis sat her down and tried to calm her. 'At this stage we think it was an accident. The driver tried to help him but … Mr Henderson died at the scene.'

Rebecca let out another loud moan. 'I can't believe it. I can't believe it.'

She suddenly got up, ran outside, vomited and cried out.

Two teachers came to her aid and brought her back inside the room. Their thoughts were also for the children. They didn't want them to witness their teacher in such distress. She was given water. One of her colleagues was holding her.

'She's in no state to drive,' said one.

'When is Tim coming home?' asked Rebecca, still sobbing.

Sgt Davis spoke. 'Mr Henderson's body has been taken for a post mortem. At this stage we don't know when his body will be released. We're so sorry, we know this must be a shock.'

Miss Johnson appeared. 'I'll take her home now. Could one of you bring her car home?'

'Yes, certainly,' said Constable Hall.

'If you could come back to the classroom with us, please. All the children have gone home. We need to collect Rebecca's things and give you her car keys.'

'Certainly.'

They all followed Miss Johnson. She and another teacher were holding Rebecca under her arms. She couldn't walk unaided.

'Where are your things, Rebecca?' asked Miss Johnson.

'In the drawer,' Rebecca replied, holding a handkerchief to her face.

They pulled out her bag and rummaged around for her keys.

'Is this them?' Rebecca nodded.

Miss Johnson handed them over. 'Thank you, Constable. You have her home address, I assume?'

Constable Hall nodded.

'Right, we'll meet you at the house.'

Rebecca had her coat around her shoulders. She was taken to the car and helped into the passenger seat. There wasn't much Miss Johnson could say to console her. Rebecca would break into heartbreaking sobs. All she could do was give her comforting touches.

They were all sitting in the kitchen. Rebecca's eyes were swollen along with a red nose from constant wiping. Someone made a pot of tea; someone held her and gave her a blanket for her shoulders. She was shivering. She wanted to see Mabel and Robert.

'They will be devastated; he was their only son,' she said, through tears and a nose that was constantly running with snot that went into her mouth unchecked.

'I've been on the phone with them, darling. They are as devastated as you. They will see you as soon as possible. At the moment they have to book a flight,' said Kathleen.

'What? What do you mean?'

'They're flying to South Australia to bring Tim back when his body is released.'

'I want to go too, please, I want to go,' begged Rebecca.

'Darling, you are in no fit state to travel. And I don't think it would be fair to them. If you go, they would also need to look after you. They'll have enough on their plate trying to deal with getting Tim home and all that it entails. You will see him when he's home, I promise. They are going to try and see you before they go. They know how much you meant to each other. They're very concerned for you,' said Kathleen.

The family doctor had been called. He arrived sooner than expected and immediately attended to Rebecca. He then drew Kathleen and Lillian aside.

'She's in shock; she can't stop shivering. It's one of the signs and there are others. I would like to give her something for sleep. She needs to let her whole body settle down or she will become ill.'

'I agree. What about you, Lillian?'

'Yes, I agree too.'

The doctor insisted on Rebecca taking her tablet. She didn't fight it. They put her to bed with a water bottle and blankets tucked around her.

'She'll probably sleep for about eight hours. If you need me call, day or night.' He gave them a card with the surgery details along with his home number as well.

They all thanked him then sat around the kitchen table talking for hours. Kathleen and Lillian took turns during the night to check on her.

'Oh Harold, I wish you were here,' Kathleen whispered to herself.

Rebecca woke up about six am. In a rush she remembered and starting wailing. Lillian ran to her with Kathleen not far behind.

'There, there, darling, you cry as much as you like. Lillian, could you make a pot of tea and we'll all sit in here with her for a while,' said Kathleen.

Lillian had no idea how to deal with this. Her hands were shaking, her head throbbed. Making a cup of tea gave her something else to think about.

The doorbell rang. It was Mabel and Robert.

'Please, come in,' said Lillian.

They looked like different people, their eyes red and tired. Mabel, who always wore tailored clothes and make-up, now wore none. Her clothes were oddly matched. She had aged overnight, as had Robert.

'We just wanted to see Rebecca before we go. We're on our way to the airport.'

'Of course, she's in her room with Mum. I've just made tea, would you like some?'

'No, thank you, Lillian, we can't stay long.'

'Right, just through there. I'll be in in a minute.'

Lillian could hear talking and more crying. She made up a tray and took it into Rebecca's bedroom. Rebecca was holding onto Mabel and still crying. They said she could see Tim as soon as they were back with him. They dragged themselves away and went to catch their plane.

On the third day Rebecca got up. She had stopped crying, only just. She felt wretched. After putting on her clothes she went to the kitchen. Kathleen was stringing beans. She had taken some time off from the shop. Lillian decided to go back to work, much to Kathleen's surprise.

'I'm going for a drive,' Rebecca stated.

Kathleen got up and put her arms around her.

'Oh, my dear, do you think you should?'

'I have to get out for a while. I just need to get out of the house.'

'Darling, I know how you feel—'

'No, you don't! No, you don't! Pat is dead, Grandpa is dead and now Tim,' she shouted. 'I loved him so much. What am I going to do? You can't possibly know how I feel.'

She rushed to the front door, then stopped and ran back and grabbed her grandmother.

'I'm so sorry, so sorry. Of course you know, of course you do, my dearest grandma. Forgive me.' She squeezed Kathleen tightly and kissed her on the cheek, ran to her car and drove to Sandy Bay Beach.

There was a wild wind on the beach that day, blowing her hair in different directions. She had taken off her shoes; her feet were freezing from the cold water lapping across her toes. Every now and then couples would pass by her. She envied them. She came here to find solace, instead, she felt her anger rising. She looked up at the clouds rolling across the sky.

'You bastard!' she shouted. 'You bastard! Why do you take the best ones? What the fuck do you want from us? How could you take my Tim? What's your grand bloody plan now?'

A man was running past. 'Are you alright?' he enquired.

'Yes, yes. Thank you. I'm upset.'

'Can I help?'

'If only you could. I'm alright.'

He looked at her for a moment to make sure, then resumed running.

Drowning herself came to mind. She found this tempting then dismissed it. It would destroy her grandmother, Tim's parents, even her mother, she thought. Finally, after a long walk she climbed back into her car and drove home.

'I'm relieved you're back,' said Kathleen when Rebecca arrived. She had been worried the whole time she was gone, fearing she might have an accident while in her fragile state.

'Miss Johnson called in to see you. She is so sorry about everything. Everyone at the school sends their love and sympathy. There's a card from them, I left it on your bed. You are not to go back until you're ready. She has organised a temporary teacher for when school resumes after the holidays. She emphasised you must take your time. Your job will be waiting for you. Now, sit down, I want to tell you something else. Mabel called. Tim's body will be released within the next two days.'

'Did he suffer?' asked Rebecca, her chin quivering.

'No, darling. He died quickly. He didn't suffer.'

She sobbed and Kathleen held her close. 'I've made some soup. You must have something to eat.'

'I don't think I can.'

'Just try for me.'

The doctor called again to see how everyone was coping. He left another sleeping tablet for Rebecca if she still couldn't sleep and a prescription for Lillian.

A further week passed before Mabel and Robert could bring their son home. His coffin was placed at a funeral parlor located at the end of the main street in North Hobart.

On the next day, the whole family gathered and walked together to view Tim's body. The weather was warm, and the sun was shining. They were thankful for it.

Rebecca stayed the longest. He looked so handsome, as if he were asleep. She stared at him for a long time and touched his cold face and held his hand. She cried and whispered she would never forget him. She had his image in a photo. She would keep it, always. She put a pair of his glasses on his face. *Another, just in case there is a God.* She wanted God to know that this was the beautiful man he had taken from them all.

The funeral was held on the following Friday. Many attended, including their uni friends, teacher's college friends, colleagues and past pupils from their primary school days. The chancellor of the university spoke about him.

'Tim had a brilliant mind and was destined to do great work in optical engineering. One of his dreams was to work on telescopes and he was especially excited and enthused after the moon landing. He was also an unassuming young man despite his brilliance; this was one of his finest qualities. He was well liked and respected throughout the university campus. Please accept my deepest sympathies to his family and Rebecca to whom he had recently proposed marriage. I can't imagine your grief. This is a dreadful tragedy and an immeasurable loss.'

At the end of the service, 'What a Wonderful World' sung by Louis Armstrong played as the casket was carried down the nave, exiting the church. Tim used to sing it all the time, especially when with Rebecca.

Many people went to the cemetery, Tim's parents, uncle, uni friends and more, but Rebecca couldn't do it. Kathleen and Lillian went with her to Mabel and Robert's place where they helped to set up the afternoon tea. It was mainly a quiet crowd. People mingled and spoke to each other but Tim's death seemed to hit them hard. He was young, his whole life before him. Most were still numb.

Robert received an update regarding the driver of the truck. He had been cleared. He wasn't drunk, he wasn't speeding, had an excellent driving record and no other convictions of any kind. It was also in his favour that he had tried to help Tim. No one, in either family, was about to pursue it any further. They believed the report. The driver subsequently wrote to both families via the Tasmanian Police. He said he knew nothing would bring back Tim and had no words to adequately express to them how sorry he was. He felt he would never be able to get into a truck again. He still had nightmares about driving. He had a family to support and was looking for a desk job. It was possible he could work at the transport company he used to drive for. An interview for the position was happening next week. He sent his sympathy and kind regards and signed it William Smith.

As far as they were all concerned, he was not to blame. It was a tragic accident.

Rebecca went back to school in March 1970. Although still missing Tim, she thought it better to be teaching. Her doctor also advised this as a way of helping her through. It was good to be in the company of her wonderful, happy pupils. Miss Johnson and the staff were kind, caring and offered to help her in whatever she needed. She couldn't thank them enough.

At the end of the year Rebecca finally accepted invitations to go out to the pub or the bistro with some of her past uni and teacher's college friends or a colleague. Sometimes she would laugh at someone's funny antics or a joke. Those around her were pleased to see her getting better.

Now and then she would visit Mabel and Robert. They were getting on as best they could. Tim was their universe; it was even harder for them. They were getting older without him, and had no prospect of grandchildren.

Time was referred to as 'after Tim'. Both sides of the family said as such. It was a year after Tim died or two years after Tim died. The shocking Tasman Bridge collapse happened five years after Tim died. And, later that year, it was five years after Tim's death that Rebecca met someone: Gary Smyth, a secondary school teacher at another school, grades four and five science. He was lively and fun and there was something about him that reminded her of Tim. Although she tried not to admit it.

She had by now moved out and was sharing a flat with another teacher from her school. Tim would come into her mind at times but she had to get on with her life, so she made an effort to not think about him as much.

Eventually she and Gary became a couple. Gary was a man who loved to test himself, liked rock climbing and scuba diving. Rebecca was happy to do the first but balked at the second. She wasn't a great swimmer and couldn't be persuaded. They both liked the movies and driving to the country. She liked reading history and he liked reading science articles. They both loved pouring over the newspapers and enjoyed each other's company.

After a year Gary came to her with a proposition. 'Let's get married,' he said, quite out of the blue.

'Um … What?'

'Let's get married. Come on, we love each other, don't we? We practically like the same things, let's get married.'

'Ah … You caught me by surprise. Can I think about it?'

'Nope,' he said opening a little box with a rather large diamond ring inside.

'Oh my goodness. How can you afford that?'

'It was my grandmother's. Mum said she would be happy for you to have it, as long as you like it, of course.'

'Like it! It's beautiful.'

'Well?'

Rebecca hesitated for a moment, then, 'Yes, I will marry you, Gary Smyth.'

They kissed. He was over the moon. Rebecca was not as over the moon, but she was happy enough.

In the spring of 1976 Rebecca and Gary Smyth married. She was twenty-eight and he twenty-nine. Rebecca looked beautiful in her long, white, slim-fitting, satin wedding gown. It was a simple design with a sash, sleeves edged in lace and matching lace along the edge of a low neckline. It was finished off with a long veil of nylon netting. Kathleen had sewn some pearls into the veil – pearls taken off her own veil she kept in a special box. She wanted Rebecca to have them.

Rebecca had one bridesmaid, a friend and colleague from school. She was dressed in a light blue satin dress with sleeves and a sash. Both carried lily of the valley with white roses.

Tears were brimming in the eyes of some in the congregation, particularly Kathleen and Mabel, for different reasons. Lillian's eyes were dry but she seemed pleased her daughter was getting married.

Rebecca had previously talked to Mabel and Robert about her upcoming wedding. They loved her and wished her well and knew she would always honour Tim's memory. 'He would want you to be happy,' they said. They accepted their invitation to attend on the day.

Dear, sweet, reliable Hector gave her away. He was the stability and stalwart of the family. Without him they would be totally lost.

It had been decided the reception be held at Gary's parents house in South Hobart, a two-story timber home with beautiful gardens and many rooms. His parents were comparatively wealthy, his father a lawyer, his mother the recipient of a substantial inheritance from an aunt. They paid for the reception while Kathleen contributed as much as she could afford. There was no doubt Imogen and Hughe Smyth liked Rebecca. In contrast, the rest of her family found them rather aloof.

'Snobby,' Kathleen whispered to Mabel while they walked around outside inspecting the exotic garden.

There were eloquent speeches and toasts raised to the happy, handsome couple. The day was a success.

Both decided on a short honeymoon in Launceston. They booked a room at Overton House, near the Tamar River. They did what honeymooners do: made love, had wonderful late breakfasts, candlelight dinners, walked around Launceston, saw the sights and had a picnic at the Gorge. Time passed quickly. It was time for them to go home.

Gary's parents had offered rooms in their spacious house for them to live in. Some of them had never been used. His parents were thanked for this consideration but neither wanted to. Instead, they had secured a single-fronted house for rent in North Hobart and paid a month in advance.

On their return they spent two days moving in with help from Gary's brother Eric and Hector. Lillian, Kathleen and Rebecca spent time setting up the kitchen, dining room and bedroom. Everyone enjoyed that weekend. There was laughter, frustration and different opinions on how things should be placed. In the end, it looked like a home.

Gary and Rebecca resumed their respective teaching jobs. Life was good.

Kathleen had turned seventy. She no longer worked a whole week at the shop. One day she asked Hector for a talk after close-up.

'Dear Hector, what would we have done without you over the years?'

'No, no, Aunty Kath, not at all. You gave me a job I love.'

'Well. I'm getting too old for this now. I want to transfer the shop to you, in your name. I want you to have it.'

'Aunt Kath, no, no. I'm not comfortable with that.'

'You will have to get used to it my dear because that is what is going to happen.'

'But—'

'I will have my solicitor draw up the papers, no argument now. I will probably still want to work here a couple of days here and there. Apparently I can get a pension, so with that and a day or two here, I can pay the bills. Lillian is a problem, I understand that. She's good at what she does but she has her days. I would ask you still keep her on for now. If she's any trouble you tell me. Alright?'

He put his arms around her. 'How do I thank you?'

'You have already done that, over and over.'

Lillian did indeed still have her days. Sometimes she was difficult to be around. Depressed, short-tempered, staying in bed for the day. Kathleen found it tiresome. Then she would brighten up, go dancing or have one of her rather odd women friends over for afternoon tea where they spoke in whispers, as if they were making some secret plan.

Kathleen decided she needed a break.

'I'm going on a bus trip to Devonport with Esta,' she announced one day to Lillian.

'Why can't I come too?'

'Because I need a break from you,' said Kathleen bluntly. 'And a word of warning: make sure you go to work. Hector will let me know if you don't.'

'You talk to me like a child.'

'That's because you behave like one. This has to stop, Lillian, is that understood?'

'How long are you going to be away?'

'A week,' said Kathleen.

Kathleen had a marvelous time with Esta and came back refreshed and feeling much better. Rebecca was there when she arrived.

'Hello, darling. What are you doing here?'

'Mum overdosed, Gran, two days after you left. Hector found her. The ambulance took her to hospital and she was pumped out. She's fine, she's asleep at the moment.'

'Oh, Rebecca, I'm so sorry you had to deal with this.'

'You don't have to apologise for anything, Gran. The hospital said she needs psychiatric help. She won't do it though. Frankly, I'd try and put her away if I could. She did this to punish you, you know that, don't you?'

'Yes, sadly I do. When she wakes up, I will talk to her. She won't do it again when I'm finished with her.'

'I've got to go, Gran. Will you be alright?'

'Of course, you go now, thank you, darling.'

Kathleen did indeed give Lillian a talking to. She threatened to tell the doctor, who may advise she be sent to a psychiatric centre. Kathleen was in a temper and Lillian knew she had gone too far.

Very occasionally Rebecca would have a bout of melancholy. It would only last a day or two at most. Gary didn't understand it. She would try and talk to him about some of the sadness she felt. He wasn't at all comforting. Instead, he told her it was in the past, that's life, things happen, she needed to get over it.

'We have good jobs, a nice house, and you have me. You should be happy.'

Most of the time she was – she just wanted to talk the rare times she wasn't.

Just two years after their wedding, it was over. Gary said she wasn't the girl he thought she was. He wanted to be with someone who was more the active type. He was moving to Western Australia where he'd been offered a teaching job. She pleaded with him but nothing was going to change his mind.

'I don't want to be with you,' he shouted at her. 'Leave me alone.'

He packed up his personal belongings, threw it all into his car and sped off. This sent Rebecca into a downward spiral. At first, she thought her life mirrored her mothers. *Am I really like her?* she wondered, frightened it might be true. *I should have tried harder to enjoy all his damn bloody outdoor things. I definitely should not have confessed my sorrow to him. He didn't like it. I shouldn't have compared him; I think he sensed it. It's my fault completely.*

Next day she went to see his mother, Imogen.

'Come in, come in,' she said 'I'll make some tea. Would you like some?'

'Yes please, thank you.'

There was a book opened on the table about English gardens. The room validated their wealth. Heavy brocade window coverings, a lush, deep couch, Edwardian chairs, an ornate glass cabinet displaying expensive pieces on its glass shelves, a grand piano proudly sitting on gold wheels in another corner, sheet music open, ready for the fingers of a maestro.

Imogen entered, carrying a silver tray containing her very best china.

'Do you take milk, sugar, one lump or two?' she asked politely with affected speech.

Rebecca noticed a slight shake of her hand, which belied her attempt of seeming completely nonplussed.

'Yes, and two lumps, please. Do you play?' Rebecca asked, making conversation.

'No, Eric does. You're here about Gary. I'm sorry, dear. I did try to talk him out of it. He's a silly boy. I'm afraid he's always looking for the next adventure. We thought he might have finally settled down when he married you. But … Well, there you are.'

Rebecca was shocked at her nonchalant attitude.

'So … um, you're telling me you knew about this?'

'Of course, he tells me everything. Look, dear, if you are here for money because he left, well—'

Rebecca was outraged. 'You think I'm here for money? I came to ask if you could help. I hoped you would encourage him to come back, give me some advice on how I could mend our marriage. You're his mother, I imagined you could give me an idea of—'

'He's not coming back, dear, he's already on his way to Western Australia.'

'Don't keep calling me dear, I'm your daughter-in-law and my name is Rebecca. Don't you dare treat me like one of your socialites.' She was very angry.

'Look, I'm sorry, I really am, but—'

'No, you're not – you couldn't give a damn. This is about you handling the matter and blaming me to all your vacuous acquaintances, no doubt. After all, you have an image to keep up, don't you? That's all you care about. Now I see how easy it was for him to leave. Neither of you have a soul, you're both heartless and Gary is just a little rich boy doing whatever he likes no matter how much he hurts others. And all this,' she pointed to the contents of the room, 'is to distract people from who you really are: an empty, pathetic woman. Here's your precious ring back.'

She set it on the table and walked out of the house, leaving Imogen rather surprised at the encounter. The visit helped Rebecca. She now felt she wasn't to blame at all; it gave her a sense of freedom.

A few weeks later she visited the family solicitor. No-fault divorce was now law. A decree nisi was issued and sent to Gary's family solicitors. There was no protest from him and after a few months a decree absolute was issued. They were officially divorced and Rebecca was now able to put this episode behind her.

The family gathered around at various times to support and console but they needn't have worried; she was glad he was out of her life. Someone at the school was looking for accommodation and came to share the house with Rebecca. It all worked out very well.

Five years went by and things had remained peaceful. Rebecca was now teaching the grade six children and preparing them for secondary school. Her love of teaching hadn't changed. She still remained single, despite constant matchmaking amongst her friends.

Hector had employed a woman for part-time work and Hector's wife, Daisy, came to work at the shop more often. There was some sadness. Hector's father died. He hadn't been well for some time. He was the last of Kathleen's brothers and now there were only two sisters left. As Hector's mother had died a year before and he had no siblings, he became even more grateful for the family he had.

Even though Kathleen was getting older she still worked the odd day at the shop and Lillian continued with the bookkeeping. Kathleen enjoyed some outings with Mabel (they had become close) and her remaining sisters. Lillian didn't quibble like she used to. Her moods were still erratic, nonetheless.

Despite her deep affection for the school and everyone in it, Rebecca was becoming restless. Up to now her whole life had been spent in Tasmania. She came across an advertisement for a temporary primary school teacher at a school in an outer suburb of Melbourne. A temporary position would do very well. She could visit another state for two years then come back when her tenure had finished.

She had a long talk with Miss Johnson, who didn't want her to leave but understood. She would give her a glowing reference, she said.

'You understand there are going to be many others after this position.'

'Yes, I do. I don't think I have much of a chance but I'd like to try. I'll miss my family and all of you but I just want to experience somewhere else. A lot has happened to me here, there are some sad memories. I need a break from it. I think it would be of benefit for me to change my location for a while.'

'Quite right,' said Miss Johnson, who admired her, not just for her teaching ability, but also her bravery.

Rebecca's only concern was her grandmother. She discussed it with her, noted it was highly unlikely she would be appointed but, just in case, she wanted to know if she would be alright.

'Darling, thank you for thinking of me but you must go and explore, try something new. I will be alright. There're plenty of people around me. Hector and Daisy, my sisters, Mabel – I'm not alone.'

'What about Mum?'

'I can handle her, always have; she's been pretty good lately. I can call on the doctor if I need to. I have to be honest, I will miss you so you need to ring me often, promise?'

'If I get the job, I promise. I'll tell Mum later.'

'Good idea.'

To her absolute surprise Rebecca landed the teacher position and was to commence in 1984 teaching the grade threes. She was excited but with some trepidation. After all, she was leaving her family, colleagues and friends behind and going to a place she had never been. But there had been many unhappy times here too. She had a deep desire to put it behind her and do something else.

On hearing about the appointment her flat mate said she would have no trouble finding someone else to share. She offered to buy the furniture but Rebecca resisted the temptation. She had every intention of coming back when her placement finished in two years.

After farewell dinners, tearful hugs and goodbyes, Rebecca drove to Devonport. She positioned her car on The Empress and had a look around the ferry. As the ferry departed, she stood on the deck and watched as the wharf disappeared then turned and watched the water. Bass Strait was calm on this crossing and she did manage some sleep in a chair.

They docked in Melbourne about twelve hours later at Station Pier. As arranged, one of the staff from the school was on the wharf holding up a card with Rebecca's name, a grey-haired woman called Lydia.

'Hello, Rebecca, lovely to meet you. How was your trip?'

'Hello, Lydia, better than I thought. Thank you for coming to meet me.'

'Not at all. My husband dropped me off so I can go with you in your car to direct you. Is that ok?'

'Perfect,' said Rebecca. 'I'm sure I would get lost if you didn't.'

Her car was rolled off the ferry and they were on their way. They chatted and Lydia pointed out some places of interest. Rebecca was concentrating on her driving, finding the pace here much faster than Hobart, with many more vehicles to navigate her way through.

After some thirty minutes of 'left here', 'right there' and 'straight ahead', they arrived. As soon as she alighted, Rebecca could smell eucalyptus trees and hear the chatter of native birds. Her immediate thought was, *This is heaven*.

'I hope you don't mind, but just as an interim arrangement you can stay here until you can find your own accommodation. I have a small, self-contained area attached to the house. My son used to live in it for a while; he doesn't need it now. Would that be alright?'

'Thank you very much, Lydia. I hope this doesn't inconvenience you.'

'Not at all. I'll take you through and you can unpack and so on. Would you like a tea or a coffee?'

'I would love a cup of tea, thank you.'

'Good, I'll leave you to it and bring your mug of tea shortly. Milk and sugar?'

'Yes please, two teaspoons.'

'Just as I like it too.' She came back shortly with a mug of tea.

'What's the material used in the house?' asked Rebecca.

'Handmade mud brick.'

'It's beautiful and I love all the exposed timber.'

'I agree. This is a community that prides itself on its art and craft too. As you can see, it's all around this house,' she said, laughing and pointing in all directions.

'The principal sent me a list of rentals available. I would like to see the agent as soon as possible, if I can.'

'Of course. They're in the main street amongst the shops. You could drive down yourself or I can take you.'

'If it's in a straight line down the street I would like to drive myself, if that's alright. Can't get lost, surely.'

'You won't,' said Lydia, smiling.

'What classes do you teach?'

'I don't, I do the administration tasks; there's just two of us in the office, it can become quite busy at times. Would you like to join us for dinner? My husband, Frederick, will be home shortly. He prefers to be called Fred, by the way.'

'I would love to, thank you.'

The next day Rebecca visited the estate agent. She looked at four properties and one of them suited her perfectly, a cottage, which was vacant and located beside a small park. The next couple of weeks were spent getting the phone and utilities connected and looking for furniture. Lydia went with her. They had fun together, finding new and used pieces. Rebecca was able to secure the basics; other bits would come later.

Lydia also showed her the school. It was set amongst the trees with a small playground. She couldn't wait to start. She had met with the principal, Mrs Joyce Tate. Rebecca learned she had come highly recommended and they were impressed with her high standards of teaching.

'Thank you, Miss Johnson,' she said to herself.

Rebecca was enjoying her new position and the school. She had done some exploring, familiarising herself with her suburb and surrounds and what Melbourne had to offer. Though still missing everyone back home, she embraced this new life.

It was evening. She was sitting outside enjoying the warm evening with a drink and a cigarette. The phone rang and she casually walked towards it. *This will be Mum making a nuisance of herself again, no doubt,* she thought.

'Hello, Bec, Hector here.'

'Hello, Hector, how are you? I wasn't expecting to hear from you,' she said, pleasantly surprised.

'Rebecca, I wish I didn't have to tell you this … Kathleen died this morning. She was putting some stock on the shelves. I heard this awful crash out the back and … well … she had dropped dead.'

'Oh, Hector, no, not Gran, not Gran.'

'I know how you must feel, so do I, we're all in shock here. Can you come? We need you.'

'I'll come as soon as I can get on a plane. How is Mum?'

'She was hysterical at first but she's holding herself together now. The doctor keeps checking up on her and one of her friends is staying at the house.'

'Alright, I'll come tomorrow. I'll let you know a time. Could you meet me at the airport?'

'Yes, I'll be there.'

'I was only speaking to her yesterday. Dear Gran, gone,' said Rebecca. She felt devastated.

'One of the most wonderful people in the world. See you tomorrow,' he said, his voice wavering.

She called the principal and Lydia. Both completely understood. She was not to worry; someone would fill in for her. Lydia offered to take her to the airport.

Hector collected her at the other end and talked her through the happenings of the previous day.

'It was so quick. One moment she was …then …' He couldn't finish.

'Where is she now?'

'At the funeral parlour. The doctor signed the death certificate. She died of a heart attack.'

'I know she was seventy-eight but I thought she would be around a lot longer.'

'Me too,' he said.

The casket was closed and this time Rebecca was not allowed to place anything next to her grandmother. So she placed her bible, her favourite flowers and a recent photo of them taken together on top of the wooden box. Then said her goodbyes to the woman who had nurtured her all her life. Her loss was incalculable.

Both of Kathleen's sisters were at the funeral. They were in their eighties and thought they would go before her. At the afternoon tea, they imparted some anecdotes about Kathleen that were quite funny, they made Rebecca laugh, even though tears sat on the brim of her eyes.

Kathleen was buried next to Harold. *They are finally together again*, thought Rebecca. She found that calming.

Lillian was still a mess and wondering how she would cope.

'Mum, I'm upset and devastated too, but you're going to have to manage. For goodness sake, you're what? Fifty-seven? You can still work with Hector, you have a home and friends who are able to keep you company. Ask one of them if they would like to share the house with you,' Rebecca said.

Lillian brightened up at this suggestion. 'Yes, that's a good idea,' she said.

Hector had been appointed as executor of Kathleen's will. Rebecca and Hector took Lillian with them to the solicitor's office to discuss it.

'Probate should be issued in about two weeks,' he said. 'All is in order with her will. I have copies for you to read as well, but I am happy to read it now too, if you wish.'

'Yes, thank you,' said Hector.

'Right, well it's pretty straight-forward. As you probably know, Hector Owen, nephew of Kathleen Whitman, has been appointed her executor. The ownership of her house is to be transferred to her granddaughter, Rebecca Parke. Her daughter, Lillian Parke, is to remain in the house as long as she wishes, providing the house remains in its current condition. If any damage does occur to the property, Rebecca Parke is to make any decision she deems fit to rectify the damage and/

or change the tenancy. All utility bills for the said property are to be forwarded to Hector Owen and myself. An account has been established to pay for them. A small amount has been set aside to be given to Lillian Parke on a weekly basis on the condition she continues to work at the grocery shop with her cousin Hector.

'When Lillian Parke reaches pension age, that is sixty-five years, payments will cease and any monies remaining will be forwarded to Hector.

'There are two vases, heirlooms of Kathleen's family, which are to be given to her remaining two sisters. Are there any questions?'

'Yes, I do,' said Lillian 'Why didn't she leave me the house? I'm her daughter. Can I fight this?'

'I'm not at liberty to provide you with her reasoning even if I was privy to it. As for fighting it, well, you can, but it would be a lengthy and costly process and you have no guarantee you would win. Might I suggest you think about your advantages? You don't have to pay for the utilities, the rates or water bills. You can stay as long as you wish and you will receive financial assistance. From my point of view, you are in a very fortunate position.'

'I am her daughter; she should have left the house to me,' said Lillian.

'What is in her will are her wishes. I am unable to address your objections or question her reasoning. Please accept my sincere condolences. I found Kathleen to be a kind and generous person. From what I hear she was treasured and respected in the community.'

He rose and shook hands with Hector and Rebecca. Lillian refused.

Hector went back to the shop. He would talk to Rebecca later. Lillian berated Rebecca for half an hour.

'I didn't ask for this house, Mum, but to be honest, I can understand her reasoning. If I were you, I would just shut up and accept it. You have alienated everyone with your errant behaviour. And, as I suggested, get one of your friends to come and share the house with you, if that's what you want. You're very fortunate. You have a place to live, a job, your bills paid – you have no reason to be angry. Frankly, it's about time you took responsibility for yourself.'

Lillian abruptly turned away and went to her bedroom. Rebecca could hear her crying and as much as she tried, she couldn't summon up any sympathy.

Rebecca and Hector were talking over a cup of tea.

'Forgive me, but I don't want to take responsibility for your mother.'

'Oh, Hector, no, of course not.'

'Well, what I suggest is this: firstly, I don't want to be a signatory for paying the bills. These will now change to your name and I think you could ask for them to be forwarded to the solicitor's address. He can fax you copies. Does the school have a fax?'

'They do. By the way, has he been paid?'

'Yes, your grandmother has provided for everything. She was a smart lady. What I can do is check on Lillian now and then and report to you if she doesn't turn up for work. If you don't mind me saying, I think your mother is quite capable of looking after herself. One thing: could you provide me with a house key in case I need to get in?'

'I'll organise all that before I go back and you are quite right about Mum. I'll be doing some thinking about my next step too. I might stay in Melbourne. If I'm here she will have an expectation that I will look after her constantly. I wouldn't have any life at all.'

'We miss you but I agree. Look what happened to Aunt Kathleen.'

Rebecca checked on her mother when she returned. She was asleep.

Rebecca spent a few more weeks in Hobart. She asked the solicitor to assist her with the utility bills and arrange with the bank to have Hector's name removed as a co-signatory. Then she visited Mabel and Robert. Without being asked they offered to visit Lillian now and then. Seeing them brought back memories and Rebecca realised she still missed Tim, still pined for him.

She spent Christmas day with her mother, Hector and his family and Kathleen's two elderly sisters. Lillian was glum but everyone ignored her and tried to enjoy the day. Rebecca's great aunts were fun to be with. They made everyone at the table laugh with their many hilarious stories.

New Year's Eve was discussed with her mother. Rebecca wanted to be back in Melbourne by then. This suited Lillian, she had invited a couple of her friends over and she was looking forward to it. The subject came up about Lillian coming to visit. Rebecca said she would see, but she had no intention of having her mother over.

On the last day of 1984, Rebecca was on her way back to Melbourne. The ever-reliable Lydia was there to pick her up.

'Thank you for this, Lydia, I appreciate it.'

'Don't mention it. How are you?'

'I'm alright. We were very close, it's an enormous loss. She was an outstanding woman in many ways and very dear to me. I've lost a few special people over the last few years.'

'I'm sorry to hear that. There is a service to help with grief, I'll give you the number, if you like. All you need to do is ring anytime and talk to a professional in this field. I believe it has helped many people.'

'Thank you, Lydia, I might do that. How is school? I did call Mrs Tate, she said everything was fine.'

'Everything is fine. Someone who used to teach with us, now retired, saved the day. The children missed you, I might add.'

'I'm so sorry, I just had to go.'

'Never say sorry about that. We all understood. We've had grandmothers and some at the school still do. Will you be able to start next year, do you think?'

'Try and keep me away. I can't wait to get back in the classroom.'

Rebecca was invited to a couple of New Years Eve parties. Normally she would accept but not this time. She spent it at home, on the deck in her favourite chair with a drink and a cigarette, listing to the music of her youth, reminiscing and mourning the loss of her grandmother.

The school year began. Rebecca was excited to be given the grade fours and working in a profession she loved. All was as well as it could be with her mother – she did keep working and had someone staying with her. Hector rang now and then to keep her informed. She called her mother once and listened to her complaints but kept the conversation short.

Six months into the school year the principal asked for a special meeting with all teachers and staff.

'I've called this meeting because I have something important to tell you. As you are aware we didn't have the intake we were hoping for this year. I've met with the Department of Education who have determined our school is to be amalgamated with the larger Gipps Primary School.'

Everyone in the room was downcast and talking amongst themselves.

One asked, 'What does this mean for all of us?'

'Well, as you know, it is local, just down the road so to speak but, sadly, it also means some of you will have to look for new positions. The school can't take you all. I will be having a meeting with the school along with the Teachers Union to see how many of you can stay on. I know parents will also be very upset, there is no doubt they will send messages of protest to the department. As soon as I have more information, I will let you know. This is a sad day.'

Everyone was affected by this news. Rebecca supposed she wouldn't be one of the teachers to be accepted at the other school, applying the last-on, first-off scenario.

Over the next few months there were many protests and discussions but the amalgamation was inevitable. Some teaching staff were called into Mrs Tate's office and would emerge in tears. Rebecca was one of them.

'I can't apologise enough, Rebecca. You were employed in good faith; this was unforeseen. We were going to offer you a permanent placement. We are all impressed with your standards and your ability to engage with the children. They love and respect you. This results in high marks from your pupils. I think you would be an asset to Gipps Primary and I have advocated for this on your behalf but, unfortunately, it's a matter of numbers; they only have a few spaces that have been filled by the longest serving here. It is not my decision to make. I'm so sorry. What will you do now?'

'Frankly, I don't know. I hadn't planned for this. Going back to Tasmania at this time is not what I want to do. Besides, I like it here. Perhaps I can apply to other schools not too far away from home. I don't want to move again; I've only just arrived,' said Rebecca, who was clearly shaken by these developments.

'I understand. I will give you a reference and include Miss Johnson's as well. I don't think you will be without a job for long.'

One evening Lydia came to see Rebecca.

'Would you like a glass of wine? I have a cask of white here.'

'Thank you, just what I need,' said Lydia.

It was another warm night so they decided to sit on the deck.

'Do you mind if I smoke? I only have one a day, out here with a drink. It relaxes me.'

'No, go ahead. I'm used to it. Fred used to smoke but he gave it up a few years ago. Not good for your health, but I'm sure you know that. I'm retiring at the end of the year, especially given the amalgamation. Fred and I want to travel around Australia. Now's as good a time as any. I thought you might like to apply for the job. I happen to know they're screaming out for administrators. I know this is not exactly what you want or are trained for but it's a good job with good renumeration plus the added advantage of staying where you are. You will already know some of the teachers and parents, of course. What do you think?'

'Dear Lydia, always saving me,' she said, smiling at her. 'It looks like, at the moment, it's my only option. I'll apply. Do you have any tips that would put me at the head of the queue?' Rebecca said cheekily.

The wine started to make the two women relax a little more. They started revealing stories from their lives. Lydia's son had died of an overdose. He stayed with them throughout his attempt at breaking the insidious habit, but to no avail. They lost him a long time ago.

'That's how I know about grief counseling,' she said.

'I'm so sorry, Lydia, that must have been horrendous.'

'It was. It's something that never quite leaves you. We have two daughters who live interstate and three grandchildren, so we feel blessed. What about you?'

Rebecca told her story about all the people she had lost. After another wine or two they shared tales of funny incidents that had happened to them, resulting in tears of a different kind running down their faces. They were still giggling while saying goodbye at the front door.

'Will you be alright walking home, Lydia?'

'I'll be fine. Thank you for a wonderful night. See you tomorrow.' She was singing to herself as she left.

The end of the school year in 1984 was accompanied by anger from some and regret by others. A goodbye lunch was held and everyone who attended tried to remain positive. Two teachers were still looking for a placement. The principal, Mrs Tate, was fortunate to have secured a teaching position but the school was on the other side of Melbourne. She and her husband were contemplating a move.

Rebecca's application for an administrative role was accepted at Gipps Primary. It was not what she really wanted but she was grateful for it. She flew to Hobart during the school holidays and spent a tiring time with her ever-complaining, avaricious mother. Her friend would come and go while Rebecca was there. It was a relief to visit Mabel and Robert who were in their late fifties and still healthy despite their broken hearts.

As usual, the shop closed for a week during the Christmas-New Year period and Rebecca was having afternoon tea with Hector and Lilly at their home.

'I'm thinking of selling. We've had a very handsome offer from one of the supermarket chains. It's only a matter of time before our current customers start gravitating to the supermarket and they think the position of the shop is very advantageous to them.'

'Goodness, Hector, that's a big decision. What would you do instead?'

'They've offered me a managerial position with them. They value my experience and my relationship with the community. It would mean we would be able to pay off our house, Rebecca, and Lilly would have more time to pursue her volunteer work.'

'Do you think they're using your good name to gain more of your loyal customers for themselves?' asked a suspicious Rebecca.

'I've thought of that and yes, more than likely, but they will anyway, eventually. The supermarket way of shopping has become attractive and popular. I'm thinking more about securing the future for my family. I'm not concerned if they are using me. Actually, it's beneficial on both sides. They've given me 'til February to decide. I am concerned about your mother here though. She'll be without a job.'

'Well, don't. I'll have a word with the solicitor, let him know about this possibility and ask that Mum might still receive the amount Gran allotted her under the new circumstances. I suspect she is getting some sort of rent from the friend who's still living there.'

'They're two of a kind,' said Hector, diplomatically.

Rebecca nodded with a look of resignation. 'I have a request. I wonder if you could both come with me to Taroona? I just want to see the house and go down the track and I would like to visit the cemetery.'

'Are you ready to do that?' asked Hector, concerned.

'Yes, I need to.'

They took her the next day. The house had been painted but nothing else had changed. The garden still looked beautiful. Hector walked ahead and Lilly held Rebecca's arm as they talked on the way down the steep track. Then they were there, on the beach, with the Derwent River quietly lapping over the rocks. It was still and quiet. The three of them stood in silence in memory of Patricia Whitman then tossed their bunches of flowers into the river. Tears where silently running down Rebecca's face. After a time, they climbed back up and looked at the house once more.

Lilly asked, 'Are you alright?'

'Yes, thank you for taking me, I wanted to go. Probably won't see it again.'

'Your mother once asked us to take her, you know.'

'Really? I didn't know that.'

'She changed her mind at the last minute.'

'I'm surprised she even asked. She always tells me how unhappy she was when they lived there. She has an annoying habit of oscillating in her decision making.'

They proceeded to the cemetery where there were more tears and sad moments.

Rebecca wanted to be back in Melbourne by New Years Eve. She gave her mother a perfunctory kiss on the cheek and quickly left. Hector took her to the airport.

'I'm very thankful for you, Hector. I hope you know that. I know Grandma and Grandpa adored and appreciated you too, every day. You've worked away in the shop through all the sad times, supporting us and putting up with Mum. If you want my opinion, I think you should accept their offer, do something for yourself and your family.'

'Aunt Kathleen gave me a start I wouldn't have had without them. I'm thankful too you know, for everything. I will accept the offer. Lilly agrees.'

'We will always remember them, won't we?'

'Always,' he said.

Back home Rebecca tidied up and went to a New Years Eve party she had been invited to. It was a lot of fun and reminded her of her student days. The next day she took Lydia for a drive to the Dandenongs. They had an understanding with each other because of their sad history. But neither was interested in self-pity and enjoyed a marvelous day in the sunshine and tea in the café located at the top.

'Are you interested in another relationship?' asked Lydia.

'No, not even thinking about it,' said Rebecca emphatically.

In no time it was the start of another school year. Lydia was right – it turned out to be a busy office. Rebecca missed teaching but this wasn't a bad alternative.

She flew down during the next school break to see how Hector was going in his new position. He was doing very well and didn't regret selling the shop, although it was an emotional moment when he closed the door for the last time. Lilly was happy to be freed-up to pursue her volunteering work with the Salvation Army.

She visited Miss Johnson and thanked her for her reference. 'You have been so kind to me. You already know I won't be returning. Just the same, I wanted to see you and thank you for everything. This school and yourself will always be in my heart. If you ever visit Melbourne, please come and see me.'

'I'm not surprised at your choices,' said Miss Johnson. 'You will always be remembered here too. I'd love to catch up with you in Melbourne someday.'

They embraced each other and said their goodbyes.

She went to see her mother but didn't stay overnight. She made an excuse of having to return to Melbourne but, in fact, stayed a couple of days in Hobart. She would always call this place her home but didn't think she would ever live here again.

The school year of 1985 was void of any dramas. Rebecca's co-workers were great to work with; they were all good friends. On a personal front, her mother was not quite as demanding and only rang three times during that year. Hector and his wife were happy with their new life. She did go down to have Christmas day with her mother, Hector and his family. Other than Hector, Mabel and Robert, there was nothing else in Hobart she missed anymore.

Another New Year's party happened along with some trips to the Victorian countryside with one of her teacher friends. Then the start of yet another busy school year. Rebecca was now thirty-eight. She had made quite a few friends and they would take her out often in the hope she would meet someone. She wasn't at all interested. Then, one evening at a pub, she met Andrew Amos, a tall, quietly spoken architect. They started a conversation and she liked him a lot. Her heart was beating faster than usual as if it had just come to life. He was five years older, obviously kind and intelligent. After all this time, with thoughts to the contrary, she was falling in love again.

Chapter 25

The Present

Rebecca was preparing for dinner. She heard Andrew talking on the phone. He hung up and came back to the kitchen.

'That was the police,' said Andrew.

'What's wrong?' Rebecca stopped her chopping.

'Well, nothing but they asked if Ms Taylor could come and see us next week.'

'Oh no … She's coming to get Meggy.'

'They didn't say that but it looks like it. What time suits? I said I'd ring them back.'

'Next Saturday, I guess, say two o'clock,' said Rebecca. She added, 'Fuck,' under her breath.

Andrew went back to the hallway and called the police.

'Yes, yes, ok, you have the address? Right, ok, we'll see her then. Thank you.'

He came back into the kitchen. 'Sorry, love … She's definitely coming next Saturday.'

Rebecca went to the little dog, which was sleeping in her basket, and picked it up.

'Couldn't we say she'd run away or something?'

'No, love, you know we can't do that, as tempting as it is. That sort of subterfuge is not us. Think about it. Even if we stooped to that kind of low, we would forever be hiding her when the doorbell rang or we took her for a walk. Not on, sorry, darling.'

'Aww,' moaned Rebecca with a pout. She kissed Meg on the head and put her back in the basket.

Andrew put his arms around her.

'Has anyone ever told you you're too honest?'

'All the time. "There goes honest Andy," they say, while I try to hide my face and remain humble.'

'Ha! You! Humble? Sure. Seriously, I'm going to miss our little Meg.'

'I know. Maybe we can think about getting another dog.'

'Maybe,' said Rebecca, not really convinced.

They were waiting for Ms Taylor. Meg had been brushed all over, her stained beard wiped with a wet cloth and a new collar put around her neck.

'You look gorgeous,' Rebecca said to little Meggy.

The dog sensed she was loved and walked back to her bed with her head held just a bit higher.

Through the front screen door, they saw a taxi pull up.

'That must be her,' said Rebecca, who was feeling anxious.

An old woman got out with the help of the driver. She had a walking stick. She was wearing a light-red, tailored pantsuit and jewellery. Andrew went to the door.

'Ms Taylor? Good afternoon, I'm Andrew Amos.'

'Good afternoon. Please, call me Mary. Sorry, I'm still a bit wobbly and slow with my walking.'

'Not at all. Can I help you?'

'Thank you, but I'm told I have to do this on my own. I have to exercise as much as possible, they tell me.'

Rebecca was standing, readying herself for the meeting. The dog suddenly got up and ran to greet Mary. 'Hello, Darling,' she said, trying to bend down to the dog. After the brief greeting the dog ran back to her bed, lay down and went to sleep.

'Hello, Ms Taylor, I'm Rebecca,' she said, rather nervously.

'Well, hello,' she said, shaking hands. 'I owe you my life, I believe.'

'I wouldn't go that far … I—'

'Oh yes, you did, no doubt about that. Do you mind if I sit?' Mary was breathless from the exertion of trying to walk. 'I still have a way to go before I completely recover, as you can see.'

'Of course, please.' Rebecca directed her to the nearest chair.

'Can I get you some water, cup of tea?' asked Andrew, acting as if he was in the company of royalty.

'Would you mind if I had both? I just have sugar in my tea.'

'Not at all, I'm quite a fan of your articles by the way.'

Rebecca gave him a 'stop fussing' look. Andrew brought her a glass of water. Mary drank it down quickly.

'I won't stay long; I've asked the taxi to wait. I just wanted to see you in person to thank you for everything you did and for looking after my dog.'

'What's her name? We didn't know what to call her,' said Rebecca.

'Darling, it's Darling.'

'Oh! We didn't think of that. We use it often, of course, not realising it actually was her name.'

'She belonged to a good neighbour of mine who named her. When she died, I looked after her dog. It's not the name I would have chosen but I wasn't about to change it.'

'Here's your cup of tea,' said Andrew in an overly formal way.

Rebecca gave him a look. 'No, no. of course not,' she said.

'I rang the school to speak to you, Rebecca. I was worried and I wanted to thank you. But I realised I wasn't up to speaking with anyone, I felt very weak and unwell. I just hung up really.'

'Oh, that was you. I thought it was my mother,' she said, with a slight laugh. 'How did you get the number?'

'You left your work and home number with the police,' said Mary.

'That's right, I did. Seeing you laying there on that day was a bit of a shock. I don't remember some of it. What happened? It's never been explained.'

'I am so sorry. Someone should have told you.'

'That's alright. We did see an item on the news, that evening, saying you were in intensive care and stable.'

'I did quite a bit of damage, apparently. I fainted, no warning, just blacked out. I woke up in hospital with medical staff all around me. I blacked out again, I believe. Later on, they told me I had fallen hard onto the pavement. I had a minor injury to my skull, a fractured pelvis, a fracture to my right arm and severe bruising. Then I had severe headaches and vomiting. The long-time medication I have to take doesn't help matters but I'm on the mend now. Neighbours were wonderful. They cooked and fussed. I also had a district nurse call in twice a week.'

'That's terrible, sorry you had to go through all of that,' said Rebecca.

'Yes, that sounds dreadful,' said Andrew. 'Are you still writing for a newspaper?'

'No, I'm retired, in my seventies now. My journalist days are over. They were exciting and heady times. Lots of stories. I hold the odd fundraising party for various causes but not at the moment, of course.

'I have something to ask. Would you mind taking care of Darling for a bit longer? As you can see, I can't properly look after myself yet, let alone a dog. I insist on paying for any expenses incurred up to now and as long as it takes for me to recover.'

'Take as long as you have to. We love her; she's become part of our family. We certainly won't accept any kind of payment,' said Rebecca.

'Well, thank you. It's a relief to see her cared for and in a safe place. Tell me a bit about yourselves. What do you do, Andrew?'

'Bit boring really … Um … Well, born and bred in Melbourne and I'm an architect. I work freelance now. It means I'm the one chasing the work but I like it that way.'

'He's being modest. He's a talented architect and very sought after,' said Rebecca, annoyed he was being so deferential.

'And you, Rebecca?'

'Um … Ok … Born and bred in Tasmania, trained as an English teacher and now working in a local school.' She wasn't going to furnish her with everything, damn it.

'Tasmania, beautiful place, I've been there a couple of times. Reported on the bushfires there in … '67.'

'Oh yes, that was a tragic day. I was at Teachers' College then. The whole university campus in Sandy Bay was nearly lost too, amongst many other properties. It was awful.'

'So, you lived in Hobart then?' asked Mary, generally interested.

'Taroona actually, just south of Hobart. Do you know it?'

There was silence. Beads of sweat appeared on Mary's forehead. She looked pale.

'Are you alright?' asked Andrew, becoming concerned.

'Yes, yes, sorry. I think I've overdone it, feeling a bit weak.'

'Let me help you up,' said Andrew, holding her under the arm and lifting her.

'Thank you, thank you. I'll be alright.' She gazed at Rebecca for a moment, as if she were studying her. 'I'd better go. Ah … Do you mind if I call you when I've improved? Come back at a time convenient for you? I would like to pick up Darling. By then I should be able to care for her.'

'Certainly,' said Rebecca, who thought she detected a tremor in Mary's voice.

Andrew walked her to the taxi, made sure she was seated, then waved goodbye. They made coffee in silence.

'What did you think of her?' asked Andrew, ending the quiet moment.

'Weird, creepy. Her voice, it's not what I expected, it's, I don't know, different.'

'You're shaking, what's wrong? I know she looks a bit strange but she's not exactly Dracula. I think she's charming and worldly, brilliant, I believe.'

'Yes, you were doing a lot of kowtowing around her. She's not the queen!'

'Not jealous are you?'

'No! It's not that!' said Rebecca. 'I felt, I dunno, I feel like she doesn't deserve it, can't explain. We're going to have to say goodbye to Meggy.'

'Come here,' he said and held her close.

Back home Mary was in turmoil and panic.

'It's got to be her, I'm sure it's her. Shit, what am I going to do? Hang on; I think there was another Rebecca in Taroona then or am I dreaming? Maybe it's not her at all. How many Rebeccas could there have been there then? Oh God. It probably is her. Shit, shit.' She was limping around the floor with her walking stick, talking to herself.

Every detail of that dreadful day was back, with intensity. The vision of Patricia on the rocks, the wind, the sea lapping around her, the paralysing fear Cecil felt, the debilitating guilt, the terror of being discovered that lasted for years. The extreme emotional pain of it all.

But, what about the life she had built since? It was a triumph, a complete success, hadn't she become a hero to some, revered by most, a celebrity? That surely had to be in her favour.

'Why am I worrying? Focus, focus, think ... Did she recognise you? I don't think so. Come to think of it, she was only about three or four then, she couldn't possibly know who I really am. Who am I, really? ... I'm Mary Taylor, I've nothing to do with Cecil Newton, nothing!'

A headache developed. She swallowed some painkillers, went to bed and tried to sleep. She tossed and turned and relived that day over and over again. Her feelings would fluctuate from contrition to self-loathing, then apathy. Surely, she was blameless.

She considered not going back to get Darling. She didn't need to; the dog was fine. She considered moving out altogether but would that be necessary?

'She doesn't know you; she doesn't have a clue who you are. Stop thinking, stop it. Do nothing.'

Despite all ponderings and justifications, guilt still remained foremost in her mind. What Mary really craved was absolution.

After many sleepless nights and brooding days, Mary decided to pick up her dog.

Chapter 26

'Rebecca! It's Mary Taylor on the phone.' Andrew's hand was over the mouthpiece and he was whispering. 'She wants to come tomorrow to pick up Meg.'

It was the middle of the afternoon. They were sitting in the lounge reading. Sometimes one of them would read a paragraph out loud, each would comment on it then resume their own book. They enjoyed these moments together.

She shrugged. 'Ok, what choice do we have?'

'Yes, that's fine, Mary, one o'clock? Sure, see you then.' He went to Rebecca and kissed her cheek. 'Sorry, love, it was inevitable.'

'I know, I know,' she said sadly.

Neither Andrew nor Rebecca slept well that night. He was concerned for her and she for little Meg.

Mark came over for lunch and a rematch of billiards with his mate. Mark was now a constable in the police force. His friend Zac had finally convinced him to join.

'Best decision I've ever made,' said Mark.

After lunch they helped clear up and went to the back room for their game.

At a little after one, Mary arrived, wearing another tailored pantsuit in light orange. Andrew went to meet her again.

'You're walking unaided now, that's great,' said Andrew.

'Yes, it was wonderful to get rid of the stick,' she said.

Rebecca was in the kitchen and the dog was still asleep.

'Hello, Rebecca. Oh, there she is.'

'She's in a deep sleep, dreaming, I think. She was making sounds and her paws were moving around.'

'Yes, she does that often. Probably dreaming of running in a field chasing the birds I imagine.'

'Would you like to sit here in the kitchen and have a cup of tea with us before you go?' asked Rebecca, dragging out the time before she had to say goodbye.

'That would be lovely. Same as before, just sugar, thank you.'

Andrew was making the teas. For a moment there was just the sound of a boiling kettle and the placing of cups. Mary was looking right at Rebecca; her smile had gone.

'I'd like to ask you something,' she said.

'Yes, sure.'

'Are you Rebecca, granddaughter of the Whitmans?'

'Yes, why do you ask?' said Rebecca, tilting her head a little.

Mary shook her head, tears started streaming down her face, her mascara staining her cheeks. 'I didn't mean it, I didn't. I was under great pressure. The apple industry was going downhill, I was losing money fast and—'

'I don't understand. What are you talking about?'

Silence then, 'I used to be Cecil Newton. Please! You have to forgive me.'

Rebecca stood up but her legs failed her. Andrew rushed to her. Kept his hand on her shoulders. He yelled out, 'Mark, Zac, come here, now!'

They rushed in.

'Zac, ring the police. Tell them we have Cecil Newton. He's wanted for questioning over the death of Patricia Whitman in 1952. Hurry! Mark, hold Ms Taylor, she's not to move.'

Rebecca was trying to get up. She wanted to punch Mary, over and over.

Mary's shoulders were moving with unrestrained weeping. 'It was an accident. I was so angry. She'd been having an affair behind my back. It had been going on for a long time. I pushed her too hard and she fell on the rocks.'

'My darling aunt thought the world of you!' said Rebecca angrily. 'I was young, but even then I could tell. There was never a hint of it. No mention of it in the family long after her death either. You bastard, you're making it up.'

'Your mother told me.'

'What?'

'Your mother told me,' she said, sobbing between speaking. 'Gave me a name, details and everything.'

'I don't believe you. You're a weak, miserable liar.' She broke free of Andrew's grasp and ran to Mary. She punched her in the face and anywhere she could find a place to hit her.

'You ruined my family, you ruined my family.'

Mary didn't attempt to protect herself from the punches.

'Rebecca! Rebecca!' Andrew was shouting at her. 'Stop! Stop it!' He dragged her away.

Mary had given up her feminine voice and was howling and sobbing loudly. It was a haunting sound that seemed to come from the very depths of her being. Her dog ran outside.

The police arrived and took Mary away. She kept howling and yelling out. 'I'm Mary Taylor, I'm not Cecil anymore. It was an accident; I didn't mean it. Please, no, no.' Then, she was gone.

Rebecca felt her strength leave her and had to sit. She was given a drink; she lit a cigarette and went outside. Andrew didn't protest. Mark lit up and sat with her. The other two brought out drinks and joined them. Little Meg jumped onto Mark's knee. No one said a word. Adrenalin and minds were still racing. Finally, Rebecca spoke. Her voice was croaky.

'It's been, what? Forty-odd years and he was out there somewhere, all this time. My poor grandparents. It killed my grandfather far too early and I'm convinced my grandmother only hung on for me. I knew there was something about that woman,' she said, pointing her finger to no one in particular. 'Felt it from the day I found her. Something in my subconscious, a recognition.' She shivered. She wiped away tears.

'Some of your knuckles are bleeding. I'll get some cream,' said Andrew.

'Funny, I didn't feel that.' Rebecca was surprised.

'Adrenalin will do that to ya. You'll feel sore later,' said Zac.

'Thank you for helping today. So grateful you were here.'

'That's our job,' said Mark, feeling proud.

She got up and kissed them both.

'Ok, let's have a look at those hands.' Andrew returned with antiseptic cream and a bandage. He caringly wound the bandage around her bleeding knuckles.

Rebecca broke down again. Kindness always did that to her. 'Andrew, thank you, thank you for being you.'

'Aww, shucks. It's nothin',' he said, attempting light humour.

After Mark and Zac left, they sat at the kitchen table.

'I'm going down to see Mum. I would be grateful if you could come with me.'

'I thought you would. There is no way I would let you go on your own,' said Andrew, concerned about the confrontation.

They flew down the following weekend and saw Hector first and told them everything that had happened. Andrew hadn't met any of Rebecca's family, including her mother.

'It's inconceivable. He'd changed to a woman? So, he's been around all this time? Frankly, I think it's better Kathleen and Harold were not around to see this. It's like one horror after another. Are you alright Rebecca?'

'I'm ok. We've got him, that's the best thing. We all thought he was dead, didn't we? Now he can rot in jail.'

It was time to confront her mother. They were expected. Andrew held her hand as they walked to the kitchen. Lillian was oblivious to what had happened. A pot of tea and biscuits sat on the table. She had aged, considerably.

'Good to finally meet you,' she said to Andrew, with a handshake. Her hand was cold. He withdrew his quickly and didn't speak.

'Please, sit down. How do you like your tea?'

'We're not here for tea and biscuits, Mum.' Rebecca's voice was stern.

'Oh, what's wrong? Has something happened to Hector?'

'No, this is about you.'

'If you want me out of here I—'

'This is about what you said to Cecil Newton the day Patricia was killed.'

'What are you talking about? He's dead. Where is this coming from? I didn't say anything to Cecil Newton. What kind of rubbish are you going on with now, Rebecca? I think you're losing your mind. Really, I—'

'Shut up.'

'Don't talk to me like that.' She turned to Andrew. 'This wife of yours has been trouble all her life, you know? She's worried me all the—'

'Shut up and listen!'

Lillian stopped speaking.

'You spoke to Cecil, just before he started going down to the beach to wait for Aunt Pat.'

'No, I didn't. Who told you that lie?' Lillian was now getting fidgety.

'He did.'

'How could he, Rebecca? He's dead!' she said with emphasis.

'No, he's not. He's been alive all this time, in disguise. He changed his sex and worked as a journalist and became quite famous.'

'I … I don't believe you.'

'And you told him Aunt Pat was having an affair. You gave him false information, you lied. Why? Why did you do that? It was so malicious, so hateful. I've always known there's something seriously wrong with you. You're sick, but never, never, did I expect you to do such a dastardly act. Have you ever felt remorse for the part you played in destroying this family? Anything? Speak up, I can't hear you.' Rebecca was now standing and looking down at her mother. She wanted to hit her.

Lillian was silent with her head down and her arms crossed. When she finally spoke, her speech was steady and lacking in emotion.

'I didn't expect he would kill her, did I? I wanted him to leave her. I was jealous of both of them. I hated Pat, she got all the attention, all the boys. No one cared about me. Not her, not Mum and Dad. They only cared about Pat and you.'

'Gran and Grandpa did everything they could for you, Mum. I know, I was there. So, what happened when Pat died? Did you jump for joy? What? What?!' she shouted in her mother's ear.

'Rebecca, that's enough, love,' said Andrew, attempting to placate her.

'I'll tell you what's going to happen now, Mum. I am going to arrange for you to go to an aged care home. You're, what, sixty-six? Someone will take you. You don't deserve to be here in this house. After that, I don't want anything to do with you again. Is that clear?'

'Yes,' Lillian said meekly.

She was crying when they left, Rebecca couldn't care less.

After checking with Rebecca, Andrew went home. She had insisted.

'You have work to do and don't forget to pick up Meggy.' He held her close before he left.

Rebecca went to the family solicitor. His son was handling the law firm now. Rebecca told him all that had happened. He found it to be an incredible story. She sat in his office while he made a few calls. There was a place available at one of the aged care homes. They were willing to take Lillian.

Rebecca and Hector packed up her personal belongings. They allowed her to take one photo of Harold and Kathleen then drove her to the home.

The manager of the home, a pleasant woman, had them sign some papers. Then they all walked Lillian to her room. It was small but had everything she needed. They unpacked her things while she sat on the bed crying. As they left one of the staff said, 'They all cry at first but she'll settle in.'

If only you knew how little I care, thought Rebecca.

Hector went back to the house with her and they prepared a few things for Rebecca to take back with her.

'Hector, please, take whatever you want from here. I'll be back next school holidays to arrange the sale of the house.' She left for Melbourne the next day.

In their spare time Hector and his wife did take a few things but gave the rest to the Salvation Army. They also arranged a sale for the very sought-after house. On her next school break, Rebecca came back to sign the papers and the deal was done. She gave some of the money to Hector and his family, even though they protested. She put the rest towards her own mortgage.

'With thanks to my dear Gran,' said Rebecca.

Chapter 27

Mary was eventually extradited to Tasmania. The policeman who brought her back was the now-nearly-retired Senior Sgt Richard Williams. He had never given up on one day finding Cecil. He was a young sergeant when he first investigated the case. This was a seminal moment for him.

Some time after, Mary was charged with manslaughter in the name of Cecil Newton and sent to a psychiatric division of the prison. She confessed to the incident but continued to claim she was innocent and really shouldn't be incarcerated. 'I was only very angry once, just once,' she would plead. 'I'm Mary Taylor now, a completely different person. I would never do something like that, never.'

The only visitors she had were her lawyer and a psychiatrist.

She also organised to have her house in Melbourne sold. 'I'll never go back there. I'll go back to Sydney when I get out of here.'

Word had spread about Cecil, his sex change and his crime. One short item on the TV news and a couple of small articles in the *Australian* and *Fleet Street* newspapers, somewhere on the back pages. There weren't many journalists around who remembered her. 'Mary who?' most asked.

The community in her neighbourhood were staggered. They only knew her as an eccentric who held fundraising parties and donated money. 'Cecil Newton? Who is he?' they exclaimed, feeling somewhat duped.

Rebecca received information six months later that Cecil had died from kidney disease. She wanted him to have suffered longer but wasn't surprised. She guessed he wouldn't last long in that place.

She and Hector talked often. He received news of Lillian sometimes and passed it on. She didn't want to say but, really, she didn't want to know. He and Lilly came to stay for a break. They talked and laughed and she showed them some of the sights of Melbourne.

'We'll come back again, maybe next year. Would that be alright?' asked Hector while they were waiting for their flight.

'Hector, my dear, you come whenever you like.' She kissed them goodbye and wished they lived nearer to her.

When she felt able, Rebecca resumed walking the same path, sometimes stopping in her favourite spot, watching the trees sway in the breeze, listening to the chattering birds. If she stayed there long enough and closed her eyes, she could hear the sound of water and see her grandfather in his garden. She would remember all those she had loved and who loved her.

I've been very lucky, she thought.

Background Readings

150 Years of Public Education, n.d., < www.libaries. tas.gov.au>

Antarctica, n.d. < https://www.naa.gov.au/learn/learning-resources/learning-resource-themes/australia-and-world/antarctica>

Change of name guide, n.d., < https://www.records.nsw.gov.au/archives/collections-and-research/guides-and-indexes/change-name-guide>

Clements, G 2006, *Tramways*, <https://www.utas.edu.au/library/companion_to_tasmanian_history/T/Tramways.htm>

Dunedin Public Libraries, Port Chalmers Public Library

Franklin, L 2019, *A History of Play: Early Childhood and Education in Tasmania*, < https://archivesandheritageblog.libraries.tas.gov.au/a-history-of-play-early-childhood-education-in-tasmania/>

Lewis, M 2013, *A History of Housing assistance in Tasmania*, < https://www.abs.gov.au/AUSSTATS/abs@.nsfb4005c38619c665aca25709000203b8d/1b052c92c38d145aca256c32002417b2!OpenDocument >*Taroona Book Digitised*, n.d., < https://taroona.tas.au/the-taroona-book/taroona-book-digitised/>

National Library of New Zealand, n.d., < https://natlib.govt.nz/>

Southland NZ Railways roll of honour board 2016, < https://nzhistory.govt.nz/media/photo/southland-nz-railways-memorial-plaque>

The 1950s – Overview 2018, < https://nzhistory.govt.nz/culture/the-1950s/overview>

Trove, n.d., < https://trove.nla.gov.au/>

Ward, G 1954, 'The Seaports of South Island New Zealand: A Comparative Study in Port Geography', Thesis, University of Canterbury, Christchurch

About the Author

Elizabeth Long was born and grew up in Hobart, Tasmania. In her late teens she moved to Melbourne, mainly to explore the experience of a bigger city. She liked it so much she stayed. 

Over the years, her working life involved administrative roles but, while satisfying, her true love has been anything to do with the arts.

She performed in many plays for the local amateur theatre company and also made large mosaic art works. Both interests resulted in winning awards. She loves art galleries, film, museums, domestic animals, wildlife and reading. Writing, however, is what she liked to do most of all. It was considered her best subject at school.

Finishing and publishing her first novel The Taroona Incident is especially gratifying. The opening three chapters had sat in a filing cabinet since 2001. During the COVID shutdowns, she retrieved the manuscript and commenced writing again.

Elizabeth likes to explore the human condition, how people cope with tragedy, and why some commit a crime. Her favourite genre is mystery / drama fiction or crime fiction.

She lives in Eltham with her husband.

My thanks to

Rosie, the Browns River History Group.

Trish, customer service, Kingborough Council.

Mark, Hobart Maritime Museum.

Dustin Moore, Network Planner, Passenger Transport, Department of State Growth – Hobart Transport.

My gratitude to

Blaise of Busybird publishing for her assistance and advice in bringing my manuscript to life. Talented editor, Anna Bilbrough, for her hard work, suggestions, wisdom and creative ideas. My husband's proofreading. My family's support in all my endeavours. And to those who took the time to read through my first manuscript:

Amanda Bradford,
Carol De Ravel,
Sue Gooch,
Monica Papp,
Sue Burns,
Stephen Fawcett

Your opinions were valued and appreciated.

www.ingramcontent.com/pod-product-compliance
Lightning Source LLC
Chambersburg PA
CBHW071200180726
48291CB00007B/2537